ESSENTIAL TOEIC VOCABULARY

看不懂的單字
不要再猜了好嗎？

1日1分鐘
新多益必考單字問題集

劉慧如 ・ 鄭苔英編著

書泉出版社

目錄

作者序

　　慧如有幸於六年前加入英語出版品的行列，一路走來，雖有波折，但總有貴人相助。在此，要感謝幾位重要的合作伙伴。首先要感謝Patrick Cowsill老師，承蒙他在合作期間，給我寫作這本書的靈感，讓本書的內容更完整。林秋芬編輯，感謝她協助我編輯上的知識，讓這本書更完善。感謝所有支持我的老師、同學及我的家人，讓我更有信心繼續寫作。

　　這本小書的誕生，慧如感謝五南出版社，及主編魏巍的大力協助，還有協同作者鄭苔英老師的指導與體諒。沒有他們，這本書絕對無法順利的與大家見面。要在多益考試中

得高分，建立全面性的英語能力十分重要，而坊間多益相關書籍也比比皆是，出版社有鑑於此，規畫了這個『1日1分鐘多益學習小書』系列，方便同學隨身攜帶，隨時研讀。在這本『1日1分鐘新多益字彙書』後，接下來還有『片語小書』及『文法小書』，也請大家拭目以待。相信這個系列的書籍可以有效率地幫助同學達到多益高分的目的。本書雖經悉心編校，但仍難免疏漏，如有錯誤或漏失，也請前輩指教。

作者　劉慧如　2010/10/12

作者序

　　想在職場脫穎而出就必需擁有超強的英語溝通能力，但是對於職場人士或想參加新多益測驗 (NEW TOEIC) 的考生而言，大家不約而同的反應就是『覺得自己英語字彙有限，尤其是對於新多益測驗的字彙認識不深』。許多人都希望可以用最快的速度並在最短時間內找到核心的字彙。

　　因此，本書在編寫之時，特別透過與職場人士的互動，匯集了最直接、最實用的字彙，並搭配與職場、時事和工作相關的例句，讓讀者能由廣泛實用的例句中，確實掌握常見的新多益核心單字，並自然運用字彙到職場中與完全掌握新多益考試字彙。

本書的完成特別感謝劉慧玲老師的共同寫作以及師大推廣部的英語班的學員們，希望在此書的幫助下，大家能跨越新多益單字障礙並且考取新多益高分。

作者　鄭苔英　2010/10/12

使用說明

　　《1日1分鐘 新多益必考單字問題集》所附贈的光碟檔案，包括了 MP3 檔案及 ePub 格式電子書。只需由電腦傳輸光碟資料到你的 MP3 播放器、iPhone、iPad 或是其他可以閱讀 ePub 電子書格式的 Android 智慧型手機，就可以隨時學習新多益各個必考的單字。配合本書紙本內的精彩內容，你一定可以快速地戰勝多益詞彙，在考試中得到理想的成績。

　　本教材所附的電子書利用 iPhone 免費的軟體 iBooks 或是 Android 手機的 Aldiko 軟體閱讀。在這邊，首先介紹本書 MP3 檔案及電子書的使用方法。

MP3 檔案使用方法

請參考圖示

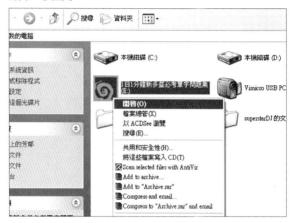

1 請先放入光碟。在光碟圖示上按下滑鼠右鍵後，選擇選單上的「開啟」。

2 開啟光碟後，可以看到 MP3 及 ePub 電子書檔。

3 打開 MP3 資料夾，可以直接在電腦上聆聽檔案。或是將音訊檔從電腦傳輸到你的 MP3 播放器。

4 現在可以隨身帶著你的 MP3 隨時學習 Toeic 單字。

ePub 電子書檔案使用方法

請參考圖示

1 請先放入光碟。在光碟除了 MP3 資料夾以外，請找到副檔名為 .epub 格式的檔案。此檔案為本書的電子書檔。

ePub 格式的電子書檔，可以在很多裝置上觀看。在電腦上可以下載很多免費的瀏覽器觀看。在 Android 智慧型手機可以用 Aldiko 閱讀軟體來觀看。本書以 iPhone 為例，介紹 ePub 電子書檔案的使用方法。

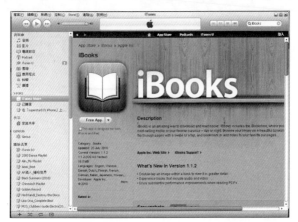

2 首先打開 iTunes，到 App Store 下載免費
的 iBooks 軟體到你的 iPhone、iPod 或是
iPad。

3 接著將光碟的檔案用滑鼠拖進 iTunes 書籍
資料庫。（如果資料庫看不見書籍的話，
也請先把檔案拖進。）

4 檔案順利拖進之後，可以在書籍的資料庫裡，看到書的檔案。

5 接著將 iPhone 連結電腦，同步 iTunes 資料庫的書籍。

6 打開 iPhone、
  iPod 或是 iPad,
  的 iBooks 軟體,
  可以看到本書的
  電子版已經在你
  手機的書櫃裡面
  了。

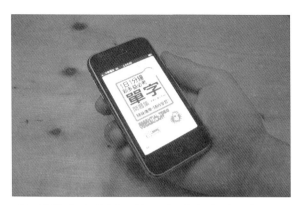

7 點擊本書縮圖，即可觀看本書電子版。

8 除了閱讀外，電子書還有放大字型、查閱、畫重點、註記的功能。

9 除了 iPhone，也可以在你 iPad 上閱讀。
以上是本書附加檔案的使用介紹。

第一部分

新多益必考單字列表

abide
[ə'baɪd]
動
遵守

The soccer players promised to abide by the rules of the contest.
這些足球球員承諾要遵守比賽規則。

access
['æksɛs]
動
取得

We need password to access these files and I don't have it.
我們需要密碼才可以取得這些檔案，而我並沒有密碼。

adamant
['ædəmənt]
形
堅持的

The board of directors are adamant that we do not discuss this with the media. It's top secret.
董事會堅持我們不和媒體討論此事，這是最高機密。

adjustable
[ə'dʒʌstəbl]
形
可調整的

In order to save space, the shopping bag is adjustable and can be folded up into a wallet's size.
為了省空間，這個購物袋是可以調整的。它可以摺成皮夾的大小。

adventurous
[əd'vɛntʃərəs]
形
有冒險精神的

Being an adventurous person, I have gone backpacking around the world alone several times.
身為一個有冒險精神的人，我獨自旅遊世界好幾次了。

alleviate
[ə'livɪˌet]
動
減輕、舒緩

Lisa's mother passed away last month and she is in great pain. As her friends, we should do something to help her alleviate her sorrow.
麗莎的母親上個月過世而她十分悲痛。作為她的朋友，我們應該做些事來幫助她減輕悲傷。

allowance
[ə'lauəns]

名

補貼、限額

People are asking the government to raise the medical deductins allowance.

人們正在要求政府提高醫療免稅額。

---

alteration
[ˌɔltə'reʃən]

名

調整

In order to avoid traffic, we're going to make several alterations to our route.

為了避免塞車,我們將在路線上做些調整。

---

announcement
[ə'naunsmənt]

名

宣布

I'd like to make an announcement. Kelly and I have decided to get married next month.

我想要宣布一件事情。凱莉和我決定於下個月結婚。

---

anorexic
[ˌænə'rɛksɪk]

形

厭食的

Being a model doesn't mean that you don't need to eat. I'm afraid that one day you will become anorexic.

作為模特兒不表示就不用吃東西。如果你不停止這種不健康的飲食,我擔心有一天會妳得厭食症。

---

ascertain
[ˌæsɚ'ten]

動

查明

After observing this plant for weeks, we ascertain that it doesn't need much water but enough sunlight.

在觀察了這株植物幾個星期後,我們發現它不需要太多水,但需要足夠的陽光。

---

assurance
[ə'ʃurəns]

名

確保

He gave me his assurance that he would finish the report by Friday.

他向我保證他星期五就會完成報告。

astronomical
[ˌæstrə'nɑmɪkl]

形
極巨大的

I never knew that credit card companies charge such astronomical interest rates.
我從來不知道信用卡公司收取極高的利息。

attain
[ə'ten]
動
獲得

He finally attained his objectives in 2010.
他終於在 2010 年達成他的目標。

audible
['ɔdəbl]

形
可以聽見的

In the noisy train station, the little girl's voice was barely audible.
在嘈雜的火車站內，這個小女孩的聲音幾乎無法被聽見。

audience
['ɔdɪəns]
名
觀眾

The audience clapped excitedly after the speech was delivered by their favorite speaker.
觀眾們在他們最喜歡的講者演講後，熱情地鼓掌拍手。

award
[ə'wɔrd]

動
授與、獎勵

Our company was lucky to be awarded the contract to build the highest building in town.
我們公司很幸運地得到了建造市裡最高建築物的合約。

bail
[bel]

動
保釋

After being arrested several times for drunk driving, even his father refused to pay the money and bail him out.
在好幾次的酒駕之後，連他的父親都拒絕付錢保釋他。

bargain
['bɑrgən]

動

討價還價、協議

Our union has been bargaining for better working conditions.

我們的工會一直在協議更好的工作環境。

barrel
['bærəl]

名

桶

The price of crude oil has gone up by $1 a barrel.

原油價格每桶已經漲了一美元。

bellwether
['bɛlˌwɛðɚ]

名

前導者

Being the bellwether in this field, this company knows that they should be very careful with every move.

身為這個行業的前導者，這個公司知道他們每一步都要走得很小心。

bias
['baɪəs]

名

偏見

As a professional reporter, you must not show any political bias.

身為一個專業記者，你一定不能有任何政治偏見。

binding
['baɪndɪŋ]

形

有約束力的

This contract is legally binding, so once you sign it, you can't break it without strong and acceptable reasons.

這個合約是有法律約束力的，你一旦簽署，除非強大且可接受的理由，你是不可以違約的。

brainwash
['brenˌwɑʃ]

動

洗腦

They're trying to brainwash us and make us believe that doing this is to help us learn to be independent.

他們在嘗試給我們洗腦，要我們相信這是為了幫我們學習獨立。

021

bruise
[bruz]
名
瘀青

I was so careless when walking down the street this afternoon that I hit a fence and got some bruises on my leg.

我今天下午走在路上時很不小心，踢到了圍欄，也在腿上留下了瘀青。

candidate
['kændədet]
名
候選人

I am sure Sandy is the best candidate for the job. She's the only person in the group who knows this field.

我認為珊蒂是這個工作最佳的候選人。她是團隊裡唯一瞭解這個範疇的人。

canoeing
[kə'nuɪŋ]
名
划獨木舟賽

My brother is on their school canoeing team.

我哥哥是他們學校獨木舟隊的。

canvass
['kænvəs]
動
遊說、兜攬生意

The candidate and his supporters are canvassing for the Republican Party.

這個候選人和他的支持者正在遊說大家投給共和黨。

cap
[kæp]
動
上限設為

People are questioning whether it's necessary to cap the contracts in the NBA.

人們質疑 NBA 合約是否應該設上限。

cautious
['kɔʃəs]
形
小心的

Being a cautious person, Nancy always thinks before she acts or talks.

南西是個謹慎小心的人，她在做任何事或說任何話前總是經過三思。

certify
['sɜtəˌfaɪ]
動
證實

He certifies that the information he has given is completely true.

他證實他所提供的消息是真實的，絕無虛假。

circumstance
['sɜkəmˌstæns]
名
情況

My supervisor thinks that I coped very well under the circumstances.

我的主管認為我在那樣的狀況下處理得很好。

compile
[kəm'paɪl]
動
彙編

Would you please compile a graph showing the sales growth?

可以請你彙整一份顯示銷售成長的圖表嗎？

complication
[ˌkampləˈkeʃən]
名
複雜的情況

Due to the complications involved in traveling during the strike, we decided to cancel the trip.

由於罷工期間旅遊情況會變得複雜，我們決定取消這次旅遊。

compromise
['kamprəˌmaɪz]
動
妥協

He compromised on his salary in order to secure his position in the company.

他在薪水上做了妥協，以保住他在公司的職位。

condone
[kən'don]
動
寬恕、縱容

I may be able to forgive adultery, but to condone it is absolutely impossible.

我也許可以原諒通姦，但是要我縱容是絕對不可能的。

conducive
[kən'dusɪv]
形
有助益的

Fresh clean air is conducive to getting rid of allergies.
新鮮和乾淨的空氣對過敏是可以改善的。

confide
[kən'faɪd]
動
信任

Most people find it difficult to find someone they can confide in and share their secrets with.
大多數的人總覺得要找到他們可以信任並能與之分享他們的祕密的人是很難的事。

congenial
[kən'dʒinɪəl]
形
志氣相投的

You and Tim are really congenial couple. You never fight with each other, right?
你和提姆真是一對意氣相投的夫妻。我相信你們一定沒有吵架過，對嗎？

conjunction
[kən'dʒʌŋkʃən]
名
合作

The police, in conjunction with the army, established order in this city.
警察和軍隊聯手建立了這個城市的秩序。

consequently
['kɑnsə,kwɛntlɪ]
副
結果地

The interviewee was very nervous, and consequently she couldn't express herself well.
這個面試者非常緊張，結果她無法好好地表達自己。

console
[kən'sol]
動
安慰

Judy's friends tried to console her but she cried for a long time anyway.
朱蒂的朋友試著安慰她，但是她哭了好久一陣子。

consolidate
[kən'salə,det]

動

合併

Our company will consolidate the accounting and finance department into one division.

我們公司要把會計部和財務部合併為一個部門。

---

contamination
[kən,tæmə'neʃən]

名

污染

The problem of air contamination in the city has become an unavoidable issue.

這個都市的空氣污染問題已經是個不可避免的議題。

---

contraption
[kən'træpʃən]

名

新奇的發明

Students from this institute have won awards for many contraptions.

這機構的學員有很多獲獎的發明。

---

contribution
[,kantrə'bjuʃən]

名

貢獻

You can never deny his contributions to this project.

你無法否認他對這項任務的貢獻。

---

copyright
['kapɪ,raɪt]

名

版權

This article is under copyright, so you can't just take it and use it as your own.

這篇文章是有版權的，你不可以把它當作自己的用。

---

copywriting
[kapɪ'raɪtɪŋ]

名

抄寫員

Copywriting is a dull occupation and it's usually not easy to find people who love doing it.

抄寫員是項無聊的工作，所以不容易找到人樂意做這份工作。

crucial
['kruʃəl]
形
重要的

This is a crucial time in your career, I hope you get that big contract.
這是你職場中重要的一刻，希望你得到那份重要的合約。

daring
['dɛrɪŋ]
形
大膽

He's so daring that he usually goes traveling in the jungle alone.
他膽子很大，總是單獨去一些叢林裡旅遊。

debut
[de'bju]
名
首播

The young man made his debut as a pianist.
這位年輕人以鋼琴師姿態首次登台。

decelerate
[di'sɛlə‚ret]
動
降低

Declining interest rates will decelerate the prices of industrial and agricultural goods.
利率降低會造成產品工業及農產品的價格下降。

decisive
[dɪ'saɪsɪv]
形
有決斷力的

When facing big life decisions, it's never easy to be decisive.
面對人生的大決定時，要有決斷力並不容易。

declaration
[‚dɛklə'reʃən]
名
宣示

The personnel manager just posted a declaration to inform all staff.
人事經理剛剛貼出一份公告通知所有同仁。

dedication
[ˌdɛdə'keʃən]
名
題辭

Our children got up and made a beautiful dedication at our anniversary.
我的孩子起身在我們的結婚週年上做了很棒的祝賀詞。

deliberate
[dɪ'lɪbərət]
形
故意的

The secretary sued her coworker because she was sure that it was a deliberate insult.
這個祕書告她的同事，因為她很確定那是故意的冒犯。

delightful
[dɪ'laɪtfəl]
形
令人愉悅的

Thank you very much for a delightful evening.
非常感謝您帶給我們愉悅的夜晚。

deplete
[dɪ'plit]
動
資源耗盡

We're afraid that the mountain's resources will soon be depleted after years of mining.
經過數年的採礦，我們擔心這座山的資源即將枯竭。

devote
[dɪ'vot]
動
投注心力

Employees in this factory are all devoted to their job. They often work overtime.
這間工廠的員工對工作很投入。他們經常超時工作。

discard
[dɪs'kɑrd]
動
拋棄

We have to discard the old furniture because it's not only dirty but also broken.
我們必須丟掉舊家具，因為它們已經又舊又髒了。

discern
[dɪ'sɝn]
動
辨識

Not all smart people are capable of discerning human nature.
並非所有聰明的人都有能力辨識人的個性。

disclose
[dɪs'kloz]
動
揭發

We have to disclose his frauds before any more people are fooled by him.
我們必須要在更多人被他欺騙前揭發他詐欺的行為。

discouragement
[dɪs'kɝɪdʒmənt]
名
洩氣、灰心

You can sense the discouragement in the letter he sent after he got kicked off the soccer team.
你可以從他被踢出足球隊後寄來的信中感受到他的洩氣與灰心。

dismiss
[dɪs'mɪs]
動
解除或卸下職務

After 30 years of service, Tim was dismissed from the company.
在 30 年的服務後，提姆被他任職的公司解雇了。

dispenser
[dɪ'spɛnsɚ]
名
販賣機

Can you get me something to drink from that Coke dispenser down the hall?
你可以在大廳盡頭的可樂販賣機幫我買點喝的嗎？

dispose
[dɪ'spoz]
動
配置

Could you help me dispose of that rotten fruit?
你可以幫我丟掉那些壞掉的水果嗎？

disregarded
[ˌdɪsrɪ'gɑrdɪd]
形
不被尊重的

The serious leaking problem shouldn't be disregarded.

這個嚴重的漏水問題不該被忽視。

distressed
[dɪ'strɛst]
形
傷心的

Maggie felt so distressed when she couldn't find her dog that she called the police for help.

當瑪姬找不到她的狗時，她覺得很傷心，所以她請警察幫忙。

diverse
[daɪ'vɝs]
形
多樣化的

Can you imagine how diverse the restaurants are in the city? You can find whatever you want to eat.

你可以想像這個城市的餐廳有多麼的多樣化嗎？你可以找到任何你想要吃的菜。

diversification
[daɪˌvɝsəfə'keʃən]
名
多樣化經營

This company is never affected by market swings because of its diversification.

這間公司因為多樣化經營，所以絕不會被市場波動影響。

divert
[daɪ'vɝt]
動
使改道

Farmers here are asking the government to help set up a system to divert water from the river to their fields.

這一區的農夫要求政府建立系統將河水導引到他們的田地裡。

dormitory
['dɔrməˌtɔrɪ]
名
宿舍

When I was in college, I lived in the campus dormitory.

當我在念大學時，我住在學校宿舍裡。

drain
[dren]
動
耗盡

Teaching all day really drains my energy.

教書一整天真是耗盡我的體力。

draught
[dræft]
形
散裝的

I prefer draught beer to bottled beer.

我喜歡散裝啤酒勝過瓶裝啤酒。

drowsy
['drauzı]
形
昏昏欲睡的

The doctor reminded him not to drive after taking the medicine because it may make him drowsy.

醫生提醒他的病人吃藥後不要開車，因為這藥可能會讓他昏昏沈沈的。

dubious
['dubıəs]
形
可疑的

Don't trust him. He has dubious intentions.

不要相信他。他的動機很可疑。

dwindle
['dwındl̩]
動
逐漸減少

The population of the small town on the mountain has dwindled to about 1,500.

這山中小鎮的人口已經逐漸減少到剩下一千五百人。

eccentric
[ık'sɛntrık]
形
古怪的

An eccentric person isn't necessaryly evil or harmful; they may just be somewhat unconventional or strange.

一個人古怪但不一定是邪惡或有害的人，他可能只是有點不符傳統或奇怪。

economize
[ɪˈkɑnəˌmaɪz]
動
節約、節省

The whole family is doing everything they can to economize their spending.
他們全家都盡可能地節省支出。

effective
[ɪˈfɛktɪv]
形
有效率的

Aloe vera can be highly effective in treating skin disorders.
蘆薈在治療皮膚疾病有很高的效率。

effectuate
[ɪˈfɛktʃʊˌet]
動
成功地完成了

The hard work of the whole team finally effectuated the successful completion of the project.
這個團隊的努力終於完成了這項計劃。

efficient
[ɪˈfɪʃənt]
形
有效率的

This department has been very efficient since the new director took over.
自從新的主任上任以來，這個部門就變得很有效率。

effusive
[ɪˈfjusɪv]
形
非常熱情的

Taiwanese people are very effusive, especially to foreigners.
台灣人是很熱情的，尤其對外國人。

eliminate
[ɪˈlɪməˌnet]
動
移除

The patient is overweight so his doctor advised him to eliminate junk food from his diet.
這位病人體重過重，所以他的醫生建議他在他的飲食中去除垃圾食物。

employment
[ɪm'plɔɪmənt]
名
雇用、職業

You can contact an employment agency to find a part-time job.
你可以聯絡職業仲介公司並找一個兼職工作。

enclose
[ɪn'kloz]
動
附件

I will enclose the latest catalog in the package I'm sending you tomorrow.
我明天寄給你東西我會附寄最新的目錄給你。

endeavor
[ɪn'dɛvɚ]
動
努力

He endeavors to keep up good performance at both school and work.
他努力維持在工作和學校上的好表現。

enmeshed
[ɛn'mɛʃt]
動
纏住

Being enmeshed in an adultery scandal, the celebrity shows no regret and says that true love overcomes all.
身陷於不倫戀醜聞的這位名人，並無悔意而且表示真愛可以克服一切。

entice
[ɪn'taɪs]
動
誘使、引誘

Students were enticed to take this course by the teacher's fun and easygoing personality.
學生被老師風趣和隨和的個性吸引而來上這堂課。

entitle
[ɪn'taɪtl]
動
使有權力

His executive position entitled him to certain courtesies rarely accorded others.
他的執行長的職位讓他享有別人罕有的特別禮遇。

equivocal
[ɪ'kwɪvəkḷ]
形
模稜兩可

I am not sure if they want to cut the deal yet. The comments of their decision-maker during the meeting were equivocal.

我不確定他們是否會達成這個協議。他們的負責人在會議上態度很模稜兩可。

---

escort
[ɪ'skɔːt]
動
護衛

When Jenny was a child, she was not allowed to go anywhere unless she was escorted.

當珍妮還是小孩子時，除非有人陪伴她，否則她不准去任何地方。

---

evasive
[ɪ'vesɪv]
形
逃避的

He didn't want to do it so he gave an evasive answer.

他不想做這件事，所以他就給了一個閃爍其詞的答案。

---

extract
[ɛks'trækt]
動
抽取，提煉

Grapeseed oil is extracted from the seeds of grapes.

葡萄籽油是從葡萄的種籽抽取提煉出來的。

---

exceed
[ɪk'sid]
動
超過

The manager reminded me that the final cost should not exceed a million dollars.

經理提醒我最後的費用不應該超過一百萬元。

---

except
[ɪk'sɛpt]
介
除了…之外

The street is empty except for a few pedestrians.

這條街除了一些路人外幾乎空無一人。

exclusion
[ɪkˈskluʒən]
名
排除在外

I think Mark's exclusion from the invitation list was intentional.
我認為馬克不在受邀名單中並不是一個錯誤。

exorbitant
[ɪgˈzɔrbətənt]
形
過分的

The exorbitant prices annoyed the customer and he insisted on complaining to the manager.
這個產品過高的價格惹惱了客人，堅持向經理抱怨。

exposure
[ɪkˈspoʒɚ]
名
曝光率

What kind of exposure do you really want? Getting more means that we'll need to spend more on advertising.
你想要什麼樣的曝光率呢？如果你還想要更多，我們就必須要花多點錢在廣告上。

extraordinary
[ɪkˈstrɔrdn̩ˌɛrɪ]
形
異常的

The extraordinary hot weather in recent days has been causing severe problems globally.
近日來異常酷熱的天氣在全球引起了嚴重問題。

extroverted
[ˈɛkstrovɚtɪd]
形
外向的

I never knew an extroverted person could be shy as well.
我從來沒有認識過一個外向的人也可以那麼樣地害羞。

fiscal
[ˈfɪskl̩]
形
會計年度的

Finally we have reached a balanced budget this fiscal year.
這個會計年度我們終於達成了收支平衡。

flatter
['flætɚ]

奉承、諂媚

Dan thought no one in the office knew him, so he felt flattered when he was invited to their party.

丹認為辦公室裡沒有人認識他,所以他受邀參加他們的宴會時感到有點受寵若驚。

force
[fɔrs]

名
力量

The little boy used all his force but the door still wouldn't open.

這位小男孩用盡了一切力氣,可是門還是緊關著。

foreclosure
[fɔrˈkloʒɚ]

名
回贖權的取消

The record level of house foreclosures in the city last year led to a mass exodus from the city.

這個城市去年的房子法拍創紀錄,導致許多人大量遷出。

forge
[fɔrdʒ]

偽造

The detective found that someone forged Dr. White's signature.

警探發現有人偽造白博士的簽名。

franchise
['fræn͵tʃaɪz]

名
經銷商

With the experience we've obtained here, we'll be able to run our own franchise soon.

藉由我們在這裡學得的經驗,我們可以很快經營我們自己的經銷商。

fraud
[frɔd]

名
詐欺罪

Recently the police arrested the biggest fraud group.

最近警察逮捕了最大的詐騙集團。

fraught
[frɔt]
形
充滿或伴隨著

Going out on a typhoon day is fraught with danger.
在颱風天出門是伴隨著危險的。

fundamental
[ˌfʌndəˈmɛntl̩]
名
基礎概念

If you really want to master math, you must start from the fundamentals.
如果你想掌握好數學，你一定要從基礎概念著手。

garner
[ˈgɑrnɚ]
動
獲得

Anthony Hopkins appeared in numerous award winning films and won several awards himself.
安東尼霍普金斯出現在很多得獎的電影，並在獲得很多獎項。

gauge
[gedʒ]
動
評估

A survey was sent out to gauge how students felt about the new uniform policy that the school announced.
一個意見調查已經被送出，評估學生們對學校發布之新的制服制度的想法。

generate
[ˈdʒɛnəˌret]
動
增加

The new company will help generate 1,500 new jobs for local people.
這家新公司將會幫助為當地人增加 1,500 個新工作。

glut
[glʌt]
名
供應過剩

Farmers are worried about having a glut of fruits and vegetables on the market.
農夫擔心市場上水果與蔬菜供應過剩。

guarantee
[ˌgærən'ti]

動

保證

I personally guarantee that you'll receive your shipment by the end of the week.

我個人保證你的貨物會在週末前送達。

handy
['hændɪ]

形

有用的

I suggest that we take some wipes with us. They could come in handy.

我建議我們帶些紙巾去吧！它們派得上用場。

harsh
[hɑrʃ]

形

苛刻的

The harsh reaction from those passengers was understandable.

旅客苛刻的反應是可理解的。

heed
[hid]

動

遵守

Students who don't heed the rules will be kicked out of the school.

不遵守規定的學生會被學校退學。

homogenous
[hə'mɑdʒənəs]

形

同種的，同質的

Scientists found that the population of the small village has remained homogenous for centuries.

科學家發現這個小村落的人口組成在好幾個世紀以來仍然維持著同質的情形。

hyphen
['haɪfən]

名

連字號

There should be a hyphen between wind and powered in wind-powered.

「風力」這個字中間應該要有一個連字號。

ignite
[ɪgˈnaɪt]
動
引起

Trust me. You don't want to light that cigarette. You'll probably ignite this dynamite if you do so.
相信我，你不會想要點那支菸。 你非常可能會引燃這個炸藥的。

imply
[ɪmˈplaɪ]
動
暗指、意指

His words clearly implied a lack of faith.
他的話中清楚地讓人感受到缺乏信心。

incentive
[ɪnˈsɛntɪv]
名
動機、鼓勵

Offering incentives can encourage workers to work harder and more efficiently.
提供誘因通常可以讓員工更努力工作而且有效率。

indulge
[ɪnˈdʌldʒ]
動
沈迷

The president has really been indulging himself in his power.
這位總裁真的十分沈迷於他的權力。

infect
[ɪnˈfɛkt]
動
傳染

Make sure that you wear a mask to school. I'm afraid your classmates will get infected with your flu.
請確認妳戴了口罩去學校。我擔心同學會被你傳染流行性感冒。

inflation
[ɪnˈfleʃən]
名
通貨膨脹

Our government seems unable to control inflation.
我們的政府似乎無法控制通貨膨脹。

innermost
['ɪnəˌmost]
形
心靈最深處

A true friend is someone who you are willing to share your innermost feelings with.
真正的朋友是你願意跟他分享心靈最深處感情的人。

innovation
[ˌɪnəˈveʃən]
名
創新力

Universities are places that foster innovation.
大學是培育創新力的地方。

inquisitive
[ɪnˈkwɪzətɪv]
形
好奇的

The reason why Allen improved quickly is because of his inquisitive mind.
艾倫可以進步如此快是因為他有求知精神。

insolvent
[ɪnˈsalvənt]
形
無清償能力的

A lot of small businesses became insolvent during the recession.
有很多小企業在經濟衰退時破產了。

insurance
[ɪnˈʃurəns]
名
保險

If you're worried about your car being stolen, you'd better buy insurance.
如果你擔心你的車子會失竊，你最好要買保險。

intuitive
[ɪnˈtuɪtɪv]
名
直覺者

He's such an intuitive that he never makes decisions based on facts but rather on feelings and intuition.
他真的是個憑直覺的人，從來都不根據事實做決定，只在乎自己的感覺與直覺。

invariable
[ɪn'vɛrɪəbl]

形
不變的

He has an invariable daily schedule.
他每天的作息一成不變。

invigorated
[ɪn'vɪɡəˌretɪd]

形
精神振奮的

My children always feel invigorated after their basketball lesson. Exercise always energizes them.
我的孩子在上完籃球課後總是感到元氣大增。運動總是讓他們提神。

jeopardize
['dʒɛpəˌdaɪz]
動
危及

I'm worried that the bad weather conditions might jeopardize our camping plans this coming weekend.
我很擔心惡劣的天候將會危及到我們本週末的露營計畫。

jettison
['dʒɛtəsn]
動
拋棄

The boss decided to jettison some parts of the business because of a staff shortage.
老闆決定要放棄一些生意因為公司員工短缺。

landscape
['lændˌskep]
名
景觀

The incinerator is a blight on the landscape.
這座焚化爐很煞風景。

leaflet
['liflət]
名
傳單

We shouldn't accept any leaflets handed out on the street. They are waste of money and useless.
我們不該在街上拿傳單。他們很浪費錢又沒用。

liquidate
['lɪkwɪ,det]
動
清算

The company has been liquidated.
這個公司已經被清算了。

lobbying
['labɪɪŋ]
名
遊說

Most governments hire lobbying firms to work for them in Washington, D.C.
很多國家雇用遊說公司在華府為他們工作。

loyalty
['lɔɪəltɪ]
名
忠誠度

The cosmetic company tries to encourage brand loyalty.
這間化妝品公司想要鼓勵品牌忠誠度。

lure
[lur]
動
吸引、誘惑

Young people tend to be lured into smoking.
年輕人很容易被誘惑抽菸。

maintenance
['mentənəns]
名
維修

The landlady hasn't done maintenance even once and the place is falling apart.
房東太太沒有提供任何維修，所以這個地方已經七零八落了。

measure
['mɛʒ&]
名
政策

We need to take emergency measures to assist the refugees from South America.
我們需要緊急措施來協助南美洲來的難民。

meddle
['mɛdl]
動
干擾、干預

Please don't mistake my concern for you as being meddling in your life.
請不要誤會我對你的關心是我想要干預你的生活。

mentor
['mɛntɔr]
名
精神導師

Mr. Hsu is my mentor who helps me in many ways.
徐老師是我的精神導師，他幫了我很多。

mount
[maunt]
動
增長

The company's debts continued to mount up.
這間公司的債務持續增加。

mudslide
['mʌd,slaɪd]
名
土石流

There were more than two hundred people injured in that severe mudslide accident on the highway.
在高速公路上發生的嚴重土石流意外造成了兩百多人受傷。

mutual
['mjutʃuəl]
形
雙方的

We won't reach any agreement unless there's a mutual understanding and trust.
除非有雙方的瞭解和信任，我們不會有任何協議。

naive
[naɪ'iv]
形
天真的

The businessman was so naive to believe that con artist.
這個商人天真地相信這個騙徒。

negotiate
[nɪˈgoʃɪˌet]

協商、談判

The robbers wanted to negotiate with the police over the hostages they held in the bank.
搶匪想利用他們在銀行裡所挾持的人質跟警方談判。

novel
[ˈnɑvl]
形
創新的

The new marketing director is full of novel ideas.
新的行銷主任有很多新點子。

nuance
[ˈnuɑns]
名
差別

The new proposal looks simple on the surface, but in fact, it has a lot more nuances than the last one.
新的提案表面上看似容易,但是它跟上個提案有不同的差別。

obstinate
[ˈɑbstənɪt]

固執的

The obstinate worker refused to get back to work until the supervisor agreed to approve his vacation.
這位固執的工作人員拒絕在他的主管批准他的假期之前回到工作崗位。

occurrence
[əˈkɝ-əns]

意外

After that unlucky occurrence, it took us one year to recover.
在那件不幸的意外後,我們花了一年才恢復過來。

omit
[oˈmɪt]

略去、省去

I was surprised to find that they omitted my name from the list for the late payment.
我很驚訝他們因為我的延遲付款而把我從名單上刪去。

oppose
[ə'poz]
動
反對

There was a campaign to oppose the building of the incinerator in the small town.
在這個小城鎮裡，有一個反對建造焚化爐的遊行。

outlet
['aut,lɛt]
名
商店

There are a lot of retail outlets downtown.
市中心有很多零售商店。

outsource
['aut,sɔrs]
動
外包

In recent years, the work of many call centers was outsourced to mainland China or India to cut labor costs.
近幾年來，很多客服中心在公司希望降低勞工成本下都外包給中國大陸或印度。

overflow
[,ovɚ'flo]
動
過剩

This outlet is going to have a sale to deal with the sudden overflow of inventory.
為應付突然過多的存貨，這間商店將舉行特賣。

overvalue
['ovɚ'vælju]
動
估價過高

If the shares are considered to be overvalued, they're unlikely to attract many investors.
如果股票被視為估價過高，那麼就不可能吸引很多投資客。

pension
['pɛnʃən]
名
退休金、撫卹金

One advantage to be a government officer is that you'll get a pension when you retire.
當公務員的一個好處就是在你退休時會有退休金。

pertain
[pəˈten]
動
附屬、有關

Could you think of a title which pertains to this article?
你可以想一個適合這篇文章的題目嗎？

pertinent
[ˈpɜ·tnənt]
形
相關的

I find that what you're talking about is not pertinent to our plans.
我發現你所說的跟我們的計畫並沒有關連。

pinpoint
[pɪnˈpɔɪnt]
動
找到

We're doing everything we can to pinpoint the problem and hopefully we will be able to resolve it soon.
我們盡全力去找出問題，希望很快可以解決。

plea
[pli]
名
訴求

The labors went on the street to make a plea to the mayor to help them protect their rights.
一些勞工走上街頭向市長訴求保障權力。

poised
[pɔɪzd]
形
穩健的

With terrific sales, our company is poised to reap record-setting profits.
擁有極好的銷售業績，我們公司穩健的收取前所未有的利潤。

ponder
[ˈpandə·]
動
思考

The chess player is pondering her next move in the game.
這位西洋棋選手正在思考他比賽的下一步。

populate
['papjə,let]

動
居住

The remote island is populated only by older fishermen.
這個偏遠的島嶼只有老漁民在居住。

potable
['potəbl]

形
可直接飲用的

Though the mayor stresses that tap water is potable, people still have doubts.
即使市長強調自來水是可以直接飲用的，人們仍然有疑慮。

pragmatic
[præg'mætɪk]

形
務實的

We need to take a more pragmatic approach and focus on getting our profits first.
我們需要更務實，而且把我們的營收放在第一位。

preclude
[prɪ'klud]

動
排除、杜絕

Her physical disability precludes her from her dream of becoming a dancer.
她身體的殘疾讓她成為舞者的夢想破滅了。

premium
['primɪəm]

名
保險金

The premiums for healthcare plans are still so high, many people can't afford them.
健保的費用還是太高，所以很多人付不起。

present
[prɪ'zɛnt]

動
呈現

He is going to present the results of the survey today.
他今天要把調查的結果呈現出來。

pretentious
[prɪˈtɛnʃəs]

形

矯飾的

When she tried to use big vocabulary words, she sounded pretentious.
當她嘗試用艱深字彙時，她聽起來很做作。

---

prior
[ˈpraɪɚ]

形

之前的

Prior to this conversation, we already had some kind of agreement.
在這個對話之前，我們已經有了某種共識。

---

privacy
[ˈpraɪvəsɪ]

名

隱私

There is not much privacy in the dormitory.
在學校宿舍內，無法有太多個人隱私。

---

procure
[prəˈkjur]

動

購置

The arms dealer was accused of procuring weapons for terrorists in Iraq.
這個軍火販賣商被控購置武器給伊拉克的恐怖份子。

---

profuse
[prəˈfjus]

形

慷慨的

This old lady is profuse in her generosity. Though she isn't wealthy, she gives a lot of money to charity.
這位老太太非常的慷慨。雖然不富裕，但她捐了很多錢做慈善工作。

---

promote
[prəˈmot]

動

升職

My boss wants to promote me to the position of supervisor of my work team.
我的老闆想要拔擢我成為我的工作小組的主任。

pundit
['pʌndɪt]

名
權威

Most political pundits are predicting that James Wang, one of the mayoral candidates, will beat the current mayor in the election.
許多政治權威預測,市長候選人詹姆士王將會在選舉中打敗現任市長。

---

quote
[kwot]

名
報價

Our company doesn't always go with the lowest quote because we think quality is more important.
我們的公司不是挑報價最低的,因為我們認為品質是更為重要的。

---

ranch
[ræntʃ]

名
農場

I dream of having have a ranch house in the western U.S.
我夢想在美國西部擁有一間牧場住宅房屋。

---

range
[rendʒ]

名
範圍

Our shop stocks a wide range of cell phones.
我們店裡有各式各樣的手機存貨。

---

rare
[rɛr]

形
稀有的

There's a law against hunting rare animals. However, some hunters are willing to take the risk for the high profit.
儘管獵捕稀有動物是被法律所禁止的,但是有一些獵人為了高額利潤仍不惜冒險。

---

rebound
[rɪ'baund]

動
反彈

Stocks of this company rebounded from an all-time low earlier this year.
今年初這個公司的股票從長期低價中反彈。

recruit
[rɪˈkrut]
名
新成員

The new recruits are all from the top universities around the country.

這些新進人員全都來自國內頂尖大學。

redeem
[rɪˈdim]
動
贖回

I can always redeem some of my shares if I need cash.

如果我需要現金，我隨時可以贖回我的股票。

refer
[rɪˈfɝ]
動
查閱

Please refer to our Website for details for all the vacancies.

所有的職缺，請查閱我們公司的網站。

refine
[rɪˈfaɪn]
動
提煉、使精緻

After twenty years of writing, I still think that my writing style needs to be refined.

寫作了二十年後，我仍然覺得我的寫作風格需要更精進。

refund
[ˈriˌfʌnd]
名
退款

The laptop computer I bought yesterday is not functioning well. I'd prefer a refund to exchanging it.

我昨天買的手提電腦功能不太正常，我寧可退款。

reiterate
[riˈɪtəˌret]
動
重申

Even though he knew there's not enough support on this issue, Mr. Wang reiterated his stance on free trade.

雖然王先生知道在這個議題上還缺乏支持，他還是重申對自由貿易的支持。

relevant
[ˈrɛləvənt]
形
有相關的

Thank you for putting these statistics together for me. These are very relevant to my study.
謝謝你幫我把這些數據彙整。他們與我的研究是有密切關係的。

relinquish
[rɪˈlɪŋkwɪʃ]
動
放棄、棄絕

If we want to close the deal, we must relinquish our previous strategy and come up with a new and workable plan.
如果我們想要敲定合約，我們一定要放棄之前的策略，同時要想出一個新而可用的計畫。

reluctant
[rɪˈlʌktənt]
形
勉強的

Though we think he'll do a good job, he's reluctant to be the leader of this research team.
雖然我們都認為他會做得很棒，但他並不太願意當這個研究小組的領導者。

render
[ˈrɛndɚ]
動
提供

A lot of people have rendered assistance to the victims of the tsunami.
很多人提供海嘯受難者協助。

repo
[ˈripo]
名
法拍

Tom's car is now a repo because he couldn't make the monthly payments.
湯姆的車現在是一台法拍車，因為他無法支付每月的應付款。

resilient
[rɪˈzɪlɪənt]
形
有適應力的

For the past ten years, Teresa Wu has overcome a personal disaster every year. She's so resilient.
特瑞莎吳在過去十年裡幾乎每年都克服個人困境。她的適應力極強。

respectively
[rɪ'spɛktɪvlɪ]

個別地

The two famous insurance companies were ranked first and second respectively by different well-known magazines.
這兩間出名的保險公司被不同的知名雜誌評鑑為第一和第二名。

resurgence
[rɪ'sɝdʒəns]

復活、復甦

Whether the resurgence of Apple accounts for the return of Steve Jobs still remains controversial.
蘋果電腦的復甦是否歸因於史帝夫 • 賈伯斯的復職仍然頗具爭議。

retain
[rɪ'ten]

慰留

Even though the university tried to retain Professor Charles for another term, he insisted on retiring.
雖然學校試著要慰留查爾斯教授再教一個學期，但他堅持退休。

retort
[rɪ'tɔrt]
動
反駁

Constantly retorting what your parents say doesn't show you're brave but unfilial.
經常對父母親回嘴並無法顯示你的勇敢，只突顯了你的不孝順。

retreat
[rɪ'trit]

撤退

When the army retreated from the city, they left all their weapons behind.
當這支隊從城市中撤退時，他們留下了所有的武器。

reverberation
[rɪ͵vɝbə'reʃən]

影響、回響

According to the paper, the new tax policy will have reverberations across the country.
根據報紙報導，新的稅制會產生全國性的影響。

reversion
[rɪ'vɝˌʒən]
名
逆轉、迴轉

No one in this court room expected there would be a reversion of the verdict of this case.
法庭上沒有人預期到這個案子的判決會有逆轉。

---

roam
[rom]
動
徘徊、閒晃

I'd like to roam about the world after I retire. After years of hard work, I really need to relax and rest.
退休後我想周遊世界。在這麼多年辛苦工作過後，我真的需要放鬆和休息。

---

scandal
['skændl]
名
醜聞

The government scandal forced the former president to step down.
政府的醜聞迫使前任總統必須辭職下台。

---

scant
[skænt]
形
微薄的

For all of her hard work, Allie only received a scant salary.
儘管愛莉的努力工作，她只有得到微薄的薪水。

---

scatter
['skætɚ]
動
散落

Please turn off the fan. My papers on the desk will be scattered by the wind.
請把電風扇關掉。我在桌上的報告會在風中散落一地。

---

secondary
['sɛkənˌdɛrɪ]
形
次要的

We think the price of the car is secondary to its safety.
我們認為這台車的價格不如安全來得重要。

shelter
['ʃɛltɚ]

避難所

We sheltered ourselves in the basement during the tornado.
在龍捲風期間我們躲在地下室避難。

shoddy
['ʃɑdɪ]
形
劣等的

A lot of shoddy construction wouldn't have been revealed if not for this earthquake.
要不是因為這個地震，有很多劣等的建築不會被揭露出來。

showcase
['ʃo,kes]
名
展示場

That beautiful Ferrari in the showcase attracts much attention.
展場中那台漂亮的法拉利跑車吸引了眾人的目光。

specialty
['spɛʃəltɪ]
名
專長、專業

This new hire's specialty is business administration.
這位新進員工的專長是企業管理。

specify
['spɛsəˌfaɪ]

詳細說明

If you want to make a claim, you have to specify the date and the place when the article was lost.
如果你要索賠，你必須詳細說明你遺失物品的時間與地點。

stagnant
['stægnənt]
形
停滯不前的

Our industrial output has been stagnant because of low investment.
因為低投資，我們的工業產值一直停滯不前。

stall [stɔl] 名 攤位	He used to run a souvenir stall in London. 他以前在倫敦經營紀念品的攤位。
stimulation [ˌstɪmjəˈleʃən] 名 鼓勵	Since there's no enough stimulation, the students often fall asleep in class. 由於沒有給予足夠的激勵，學生經常在課堂上打瞌睡。
stimulus [ˈstɪmjələs] 形 激勵與刺激	The mayors are looking for a stimulus package to pass before the upcoming election. 市長們在尋找一個有激勵的提案在將臨的選舉前通過。
stockpile [ˈstɑkˌpaɪl] 動 囤積	Before the typhoon came, Mother was stockpiling bottled water and instant noodles. 在颱風到來之前，媽媽囤積瓶裝水和泡麵。
stopover [ˈstɑpˌovɚ] 名 轉機	My ticket to the UK includes a stopover for one night in Amsterdam. 我到英國的機票包含在阿姆斯特丹轉機停留一晚。
strap [stræp] 名 帶子	You don't want to get rid of those straps. You can clip things on to them. 你不需要把那些帶子拿掉的。你可以把東西夾在上面。

struggling
[ˈstrʌɡlɪŋ]
形
為生計掙扎的

When Leon was still a struggling singer, he paid the bills by selling cell phones.
當里昂仍然是個為生計掙扎的歌星時，他賣手機來支付他的帳單。

subjective
[səbˈdʒɛktɪv]
形
主觀的

The judge asked the jury not to be subjective but to come up with a verdict based on the evidence.
法官要求陪審團不要主觀，要按照證據來進行裁決。

subscription
[səbˈskrɪpʃən]
名
訂閱費、會費

I have to pay my subscription this week.
我這個星期需要繳訂閱費。

subsidize
[ˈsʌbsəˌdaɪz]
動
補貼

The government plans to use $36 billion to subsidize locally issued bonds for school construction.
政府已有計畫使用三百六十億地方債券來補助學校建設。

substantial
[səbˈstænʃəl]
形
實質上、大體上

The substantial impact from this construction will be good both financially and environmentally.
這個工程的實質影響將會在財務上的和環境上有助益。

substantiate
[səbˈstænʃɪˌet]
動
證實

If you can't substantiate your claim in a court of law, we might lose the case.
如果你無法在法院內證實你的說詞，我們將會輸掉這場官司。

surmise
[sə-'maɪz]
動
臆測

I surmise that under the circumstances, he'll definitely choose to keep silent.
我推測在這種狀況下，他絕對不會選擇沈默。

switch
[swɪtʃ]
動
轉換

Please wait until the lights have switched to green.
請等燈號變成綠燈。

synopsis
[sɪ'nɑpsɪs]
名
大綱、大意

I need to compile a synopsis of my three latest research results and send it to my advisor.
我需要彙整我最近三篇研究報告的大綱，並送交給我的指導教授。

teeming
['timɪŋ]
形
擠滿的

This old market is always teeming with people on the weekend.
這個老市場在週末總擠滿了人。

tempt
[tɛmpt]
動
引誘

Though she knows I don't like fruits, she still tried to tempt me to eat the orange.
雖然她知道我不喜歡水果，她仍然設法引誘我吃柳橙。

tenure
['tɛnjə-]
名
任期

Recent research found that the average tenure of a CEO president in this field is 5 years.
近期的研究告訴我們在這個行業裡的執行長任期平均是五年。

touchy
['tʌtʃɪ]

棘手的、易怒的

As he's become very touchy these days, we need to be careful when talking with him.

由於他最近變得非常易怒，我們跟他說話時需要小心些。

tough
[tʌf]

堅強的

My mother is a tough woman who brought up four children by herself.

我的母親是位堅強的女士，她自己帶大四個孩子。

tricky
['trɪkɪ]

有陷阱的

Paul found that some of the questions on the final exam were tricky, but he nonetheless felt quite confident.

保羅發現期末考有些題目是有陷阱的，不過他寫得很有信心。

ultimate
['ʌltəmɪt]

絕對的

This request is from the ultimate authority and no one here will be exempt.

這個命令是來自最高層級，沒有人可以豁免。

unconscious
[ʌn'kɑnʃəs]

不省人事的

The unconscious abused child was sent to the hospital in the middle of the night.

這個昏迷的受虐小孩在半夜裡被送到醫院。

unveil
[ʌn'vel]

上市

After Apple unveiled its new product, many problems have been reported with it.

在蘋果公司的新產品上市後，針對此產品的問題不斷地被報導。

vacant
['vekənt]
形
空著的

The house has been vacant since the last tenant moved out.

這間房子自從前一位房客搬走後一直空著。

valid
['vælɪd]
形
有效的

I doubt if these reports are valid. The figures look a little strange to me.

我不確定這些報告是有效的。這些數字在我看起來很奇怪。

volatile
['vɑlətl]
形
多變的

The political situation in Thailand has been volatile.

泰國的政治情勢一直是詭譎多變。

whereas
[wɛr'æz]
連
但

Her supervisor is easygoing, whereas mine is tough to work with.

她的上司是個容易相處的人,而我的上司卻是個難對付的棘手人物。

which
[wɪtʃ]
形
哪一個

I don't know which one to choose because they are all beautiful.

我不知道要選哪一個因為它們都很漂亮。

yield
[jild]
動
讓路

When driving on the street, you have to yield to oncoming cars.

在路上開車時,你必須讓路給來車。

第二部分

新多益必考單字問題集

問題 001

What's the _____ between high prices and inflation?

(A) coordination

(B) correlation

(C) combination

問題 002

Mark is just a business _____ so I don't know him very well.

(A) acquaintance

(B) seminar

(C) journalist

問題 001 解答 (B) correlation 關連

解答 高物價與通貨膨脹之間的**關係**為何？

選項 (A) 協調溝通 (B) 關連 (C) 組合

補充例句

coordination (n.) 協調溝通
Jammy is doing an incredible coordination job between departments.

傑米把各部門的協調溝通工作做得很好。

combination (n.) 組合
It's a combination of several reasons for me wearing your dress, and one of them is because I haven't done laundry for weeks.

我之所以穿你的衣服有諸多原因，其中之一是我已經好幾週沒洗衣服了。

問題 002 解答 (A) acquaintance 認識的人

解答 馬克只是一個職場**認識的人**，所以我跟他不熟。

選項 (A) 認識的人 (B) 研討會 (C) 記者

補充例句

seminar (n.) 研討會
The seminar we are holding this week is going to last for 5 days.

我們這星期要辦的研討會將會持續五天。

journalist (n.) 記者
It's essential to be impartial when you are a journalist.

當一個記者基本的是需要沒有偏見。

問題 003

In the past, only the _____ people were able to have their children educated or have tutors.

      (A) open minded

      (B) affectionate

      (C) affluent

問題 004

This year a lot of companies are trying to _____ by not hiring new staff.

      (A) impede

      (B) economize

      (C) facilitate

問題 003 解答 (C) affluent 富裕的

解答 在以前，只有**富裕的**人家才有能力讓孩子受教育或聘請家庭教師。

選項 (A) 開明的　(B) 熱情的　(C) 富裕的

補充例句

open minded (adj.) 開明的
Sarah's got such open minded parents who let her decide what she wants to do study in university.

莎拉的父母很開明， 他們讓她自己決定大學要學什麼。

affectionate (adj.) 熱情的
Emma, my niece, just gave me an affectionate embrace which made me really happy to feel welcomed.

我姪女愛瑪給了我一個熱情的擁抱，讓我因爲感到受歡迎而開心。

問題 004 解答 (C) economize 節約

解答 今年有很多公司試圖藉由不雇用新員工來節省財源。

選項 (A) 阻礙　(B) 節約　(C) 幫助

補充例句

impede (v.) 阻礙
His lack of experiences in this professional is impeding his chances of finding a better job.

他在這個專業上缺乏經驗，阻礙他找到一個更好的工作的機會。

facilitate (v.) 幫助
There are a lot of ways to facilitate this plan going forward so don't worry about it.

有很多方式可以協助這個計畫進行，所以不用擔心。

問題 005

Flying by corporate jet is considered _____ that the whole world frowns upon right now.

(A) extravagant

(B) extrapolation

(C) extended

問題 006

They need to come up with new ideas soon since none of the plans are _____ at the moment.

(A) scant

(B) feasible

(C) legible

問題 005 解答 (A) extravagant 浪費的

解答 搭乘公司專機被認為是**浪費**，全世界都在撻伐。

選項 (A) 浪費的　(B) 推斷　(C) 延伸的

補充例句

extrapolation (n.) 推斷
I assume that's just an extrapolation unless you have any solid proof to convince me.

我認為這只是個推論，除非你有任何確鑿的證據可以說服我。

extended (adj.) 延伸的
Only recent have men come to realize that unless freedom is universal it is only extended privilege.

直到最近人們才理解除非自由國際化了，不然它只是延伸的福利。

問題 006 解答 (B) feasible 可實行的

解答 他們必須很快地想出一些新的意見，因為目前沒有一個計畫是**可行**的。

選項 (A) 微薄的　(B) 可實行的　(C) 清楚的

補充例句

scant (adj.) 微薄的
When people pay scant attention to discussions that have importance to their work and their decisions, they risk faulty judgments.

當人們較少注意到跟工作相關的重要討論與決定，他們即冒著錯誤判斷的風險。

legible (adj.) 清楚的
His signature is barely legible.

他的簽名幾乎是無法辨識的。

問題 007

According to the committee, there's going to be a _____ to Mr. Franksome's outstanding performance in the movie industry.

      (A) recognition

      (B) ceremony

      (C) tribute

問題 008

We have to elbow our way through the _____ station during rush hours.

      (A) teeming

      (B) abundant

      (C) persistent

解答 根據委員會說法，將會有個**表揚**讚許富藍克森先生在
電影界的傑出表現。

選項 (A) 承認　(B) 典禮　(C) 頌辭

補充例句

recognition (n.) 承認
Mary takes this promotion as the recognition of her
exceptional performance at work.

瑪麗將公司給她的升遷視爲對她在工作上傑出表現的認可。

ceremony (n.) 典禮
The ceremony was a total disaster because of the sudden
storm.

這個典禮因爲突然的暴雨而完全成了災難。

解答 在尖峰時間，我們必須從**擁擠的**車站中擠過去。

選項 (A) 擁擠的　(B) 豐富的　(C) 持續的

補充例句

abundant (adj.) 豐富的
Our company has abundant supplies of goods you are looking
for.

我們公司有足夠的物品來滿足你們的需求。

persistent (adj.) 持續的
There have been persistent rumors that the president is going
to resign.

持續有謠言說總裁就快要辭職了。

問題 009

Many companies are _____ to reduce carbon emissions.

(A) preparing

(B) resenting

(C) pledging

問題 010

For the time being, we want to avoid any _____ of this agreement to the media.

(A) alteration

(B) nuance

(C) leakage

解答 很多公司都**宣示要**降低碳排放量。

選項 (A) 準備 (B) 憎恨的 (C) 誓言做到

補充例句

prepare (v.) 準備
We only have a few hours to prepare for the meeting this afternoon.

我們只有幾個小時可以準備今天下午的會議。

resent (v.) 憎恨的
One who resents the responsibilities that being put upon would never make obvious progress.

憎恨被賦予責任的人不會有明顯的進步。

解答 目前為止，我們要避免**洩漏**任何合約的消息給媒體。

選項 (A) 調整 (B) 些許差別 (C) 洩漏

補充例句

alteration (n.) 調整
We would like to inform you that there has been an alteration in our plans.

我們想要告訴您，我們的計畫已有了調整。

nuance (n.) 些許差別
The actor is so highly acclaimed because he is able to convey the slightest nuance of emotion with only his eyes.

這個演員之所以受到高度讚賞，是因為他能夠只用眼神就傳達出些微不同的情感。

問題 011

Stock market recently has been _____ because of the unstable economy policy from the government.

       (A) emerging

       (B) fluctuating

       (C) prejudicing

問題 012

After losing an important customer, his chances of promotion are seriously _____ .

       (A) jeopardized

       (B) dominated

       (C) canceled

問題 011 解答 (B) fluctuating 浮動

解答 因為政府不確定的經濟政策，股市最近**浮動不穩**。

選項 (A) 出現、浮現 (B) 浮動 (C) 偏見

補充例句

emerge (v.) 出現、浮現
All I'm asking for is a little patience. I truly believe that the facts will eventually emerge.

我只要求一點點耐性。我真的相信真相終究會水落石出。

prejudice (n.) 偏見
Prejudice sometimes results in discrimination especially when it comes to race problem.

偏見有時候會形成歧視，尤其是跟種族問題相關時。

問題 012 解答 (A) jeopardized 危及

解答 失去了重要的客戶以後，他晉升的機會就嚴重**受到危害**了。

選項 (A) 危及 (B) 主導 (C) 取消

補充例句

dominate (v.) 主導
China seems to dominate the world economically.

中國似乎主導著世界經濟。

cancel (v.) 取消
Tim canceled the meeting at the last moment.

提姆在最後一刻取消了會議。

問題 013

The official government _____ of the tax increase will come out after it's approved by the Legislator Yuan.

(A) notification

(B) informant

(C) pronouncement

問題 014

A _____ between the two well-known companies will help make them a leader in the world.

(A) merger

(B) mandate

(C) measure

解答　政府漲稅的**正式公告**在立法院通過後會發布。

選項　(A) 通知　(B) 線民　(C) 官方公告

補充例句

notification (n.) 通知
Have you checked out the notification on the bulletin board?
你看了公布欄上的通知嗎？

informant (n.) 線民
Being an informant of the Police, Timothy secretly helped fight against crime.
作為警察的線民，提摩西祕密地幫助他們打擊罪犯。

解答　這兩間有名公司的**合併**，將會讓它們變成世界的領導者。

選項　(A) 合併　(B) 授權　(C) 手段

補充例句

mandate (n.) 授權
A new quality mandate has been sent down; everyone must follow the strictest quality control now.
上層已經下達一個新的品質標準，現在每個人都必須遵照嚴格的品管。

measure (n.) 方法
This car companies design these measures to guarantee car safety.
這家汽車公司設計這些方法來保證車輛的安全。

The big amount of _____ on the proposal surprised the president and he decided to put it off first. In the meantime, he wants to seek for more support.

(A) compliment

(B) backlash

(C) preservation

The journalist picked up the interviewees on the street _____ .

(A) generally

(B) randomly

(C) alphabetically

問題 015 解答　(B) backlash 強烈反對

解答　針對這個提案而來的**強烈反對**讓總統驚訝，因此他決定先延期。同時，他也希望尋求更多支持。

選項　(A) 稱許　(B) 強烈反對　(C) 維護

補充例句

compliment (n.)　稱許
Parents should be generous when giving children compliments because it's the best way to bring out the best of them.

父母應該很慷慨地給予孩子讚許，因為這是讓他們表現佳的最好方法。

preservation (n.)　維護
If you want to eat healthily, the preservation of food can be a crucial thing during hot summer days.

如果你想要吃得健康，在酷熱夏天時食物的保存是非常重要的。

問題 016 解答　(B) randomly 隨機地

解答　記者在街上**隨機地**選擇受訪的對象。

選項　(A) 一般地　(B) 隨機地　(C) 按照字母地

補充例句

generally (adv.)　一般地
Generally speaking, the majority of people in Taiwan like to drink tea.

一般而言，大部分的台灣人喜歡喝茶。

alphabetically (adv.)　按照字母地
All the authors' names are arranged alphabetically.

所有作者的名字都是按照字母順序排列的。

After _____ his Master's degree in Art, he decided to apply for a teaching position at an elementary school.

(A) attaining

(B) sustaining

(C) persisting

The new hirer has a lot of marketing _____ so she is going to be a big help to the department.

(A) audit

(B) critic

(C) savvy

解答 在**取得**碩士學位後，他決定在一所小學申請教職。

選項 (A) 取得 (B) 支撐 (C) 堅持

補充例句

sustaining (sustain) (v.) 支撐

In order to sustain a certain level of living quality, the mother decided to take a part time job to assist the father.

爲了維持一定的生活水準，母親決定找一份兼職工作來幫助父親。

persisting (persist) (v.) 堅持

In spite of the opposing opinions, the company remains persisting on the "Uniform on Wednesday" policy.

儘管有許多反對的意見，公司仍然堅持「週三穿制服」的政策。

解答 這位新聘員工有很多行銷**知識**，所以她必能成為此部門的得力助手。

選項 (A) 稽查 (B) 評論 (C) 通曉

補充例句

audit (n.) 稽查

Our company is subject to regular financial audits.

我們公司必須有經常性的財務稽核。

critic (n.) 評論者

The movie was viewed as a disaster because all critics hated it.

這部電影被視爲災難，因爲所有的評論者都討厭它。

問題 019

The company just spent a considerate amount of money on the _____ of several buildings.

        (A) acquisitions

        (B) delusions

        (C) requisitions

問題 020

The flight attendants show the passengers how to _____ themselves in case of a crash landing.

        (A) bail

        (B) mount

        (C) brace

問題 019 解答 (A) acquisitions 取得、收購

解答 公司剛剛花了一大筆錢在**購置**大樓上。

選項 (A) 取得、收購　(B) 迷惑、妄想　(C) 要求

補充例句

delusion (n.) 迷惑、妄想
Sam suffers from delusions and often thinks he is a VIP of a club.

山姆受妄想症之苦，且經常以為自己是某俱樂部的重要人物。

requisition (n.) 要求
The officer in-charge issued a requisition to the townspeople for food and water.

負責的軍官對鎮民發布徵收食物與水的要求。

問題 020 解答 (C) brace 防範

解答 空服員示範旅客如何在飛機迫降時做**防範**。

選項 (A) 保釋　(B) 攀升　(C) 防範

補充例句

bail (v.) 保釋、紓困
Dr. Watson bailed Sherlock Holmes out of jail.

華生醫生將福爾摩斯從監獄保釋出來。

mount (v.) 攀升
The prices of real estate have mounted rapidly in recent years.

近年來房地產價格攀升得相當快速。

Patricia wants to finish her Master's degree in two years; therefore, she _____ in her study all day and all night.

> (A) puts
>
> (B) immerses
>
> (C) indulges

The gold bracelet that Chandler wears is quite _____.

> (A) colloquial
>
> (B) ostentatious
>
> (C) effective

問題 021 解答 (B) immerses 埋首於

解答 派翠莎想要在兩年內取得碩士學位，所以整日整夜都**埋首於**書堆裡。

選項 (A) 放置 (B) 埋首於 (C) 沉溺於

補充例句

put (v.) 放置
Can we put off this issue until next time?
此議題我們可以延到下次再談嗎？

indulge (v.) 沉溺於
Tommy's worried about his youngest son because he indulges in video games all day and he sometimes even skips school.
湯米十分擔心他的小兒子，因為他沉迷於電腦遊戲，有時還會蹺課。

問題 022 解答 (B) ostentatious 浮誇的

解答 錢德勒戴的黃金手鍊太**浮誇**了。

選項 (A) 口語的 (B) 浮誇的 (C) 有效的

補充例句

colloquial (adj.) 口語的
My supervisor pointed out that the phrases were too colloquial to use in formal emails.
我的上司指出這些用語太過口語而不適合用在正式的電子郵件中。

effective (adj.) 有效率的
The painkiller is an extremely effective cure for a headache.
這個止痛藥對於頭痛非常有效。

問題 023

Paris has been the _____ of fashion industry for centuries.

      (A) pundit

      (B) bellwether

      (C) preceptor

問題 024

A trustee is appointed to _____ the bankrupt company's assets and the money is used to pay off the debts.

      (A) liquidate

      (B) consolidate

      (C) scatter

問題 023 解答 (B) bellwether 先驅者

解答 巴黎穩坐時尚企業之**先驅**已經幾世紀了。

選項 (A) 權威 (B) 先驅者 (C) 指導教授

補充例句

pundit (n.) 權威

Some business pundits claim that the only way to attract foreign investors is to stabilize both political and economic situation.

一些商業權威表示，唯一可以吸引外國投資者的方法就是讓政局和經濟穩定。

preceptor (n.) 指導教授

Doctor Robinson was my preceptor when I was still an intern at the hospital.

當我還是醫院裡的實習醫生時，羅賓森醫生是我的指導教授。

問題 024 解答 (A) liquidate 清算

解答 財產受託管理人被指派來**清算**這間破產公司的資產，並運用此財產來償付債務。

選項 (A) 清算 (B) 合併 (C) 散開

補充例句

consolidate (v.) 合併

Several local businesses have consolidated to form a large company in order to survive.

幾個當地的公司為了生存合併成為一間大的公司。

scatter (v.) 散開

The sparrows scattered right away when they saw my dog running toward them.

這些麻雀在我的小狗跑向牠們時，就馬上散開了。

問題 025

As there's a drought expected, people are _____ bottled water which has caused the rise of the price.

(A) stockpiling

(B) escalating

(C) exchanging

問題 026

My company has an _____ at the end of each fiscal year.

(A) assurance

(B) emission

(C) audit

解答 由於乾旱預測，人們都在**囤積**瓶裝水，因此也造成了價格上漲。

選項 (A) 囤積　(B) 擴張　(C) 交換

補充例句

escalating (escalate) (v.) 擴張
Damages of the tsunami accident are escalating.

海嘯造成的損害正在擴大。

exchanging (exchange) (v.) 交換
Every year, at least over 1000 students are benefited from the student exchange program.

每年，至少有一千名學生因為交換學生方案而受惠。

解答 我們公司在每個會計年度結束時都會有**稽核**。

選項 (A) 保證　(B) 排放氣體　(C) 稽查

補充例句

assurance (n.) 保證
He gave me his assurance that he would remit me the money right away.

他向我保證他會馬上把錢匯給我。

emission (n.) 排放氣體
There are more and more regulations which require a reduction in harmful emissions.

有越來越多的規定，要求減少有害氣體的排放。

As expected, the economic situation is getting better and the _____ are up. As a result, we will soon be able to hire back the staff we laid off last years.

(A) overheads

(B) tensions

(C) revenues

Most companies try to keep their losses to a _____ . They believe the economy will start to turn around soon.

(A) candidate

(B) trainee

(C) minimal

問題 027 解答 (C) revenues 收入

解答 如同預期的，經濟狀況好轉了，而我們的**收入**也增加。其結果是，我們將很快可以回聘去年遣散的同事。

選項 (A) 固定開銷　(B) 緊張氣氛　(C) 收入

補充例句

overhead (n.) 固定開銷
Comparing the overhead between a shop and a stand, they decided to go for the latter one because it would be a lot easier to start with.

比較了店鋪和地攤的固定開銷，他們決定要擺地攤，因為比較容易開始。

tension (n.) 緊張氣氛
The tension between two teams are getting worse.
兩隊之間的緊張氣氛越來越高漲。

問題 028 解答 (C) minimal 最低的

解答 大部分的公司試著把損失降到**最低**。他們相信經濟很快就會好轉。

選項 (A) 候選人　(B) 實習者　(C) 最低的

補充例句

candidate (n.) 候選人
The candidate accused the police of being racist and violating election laws.

這位候選人控告警方是種族主義者，並且違反選舉法。

trainee (n.) 實習者
The new trainee will be under your direction.
這個新的實習者將歸你所管。

問題 029

Kenneth was very upset when he was told that he would be _____ due to the fact that he failed to reach the target of this season.

(A) degenerated

(B) delighted

(C) degraded

問題 030

They need to _____ their business model to achieve success.

(A) tweak

(B) clog

(C) highlight

問題 029 解答 (C) degraded 降級

解答 當肯尼司被告知因為沒達到本季目標而將要被**降級**時，他非常難過。

選項 (A) 墮落的、減低的　(B) 開心愉悅的　(C) 降級

補充例句

degenerated (degenerate) (v.) 墮落的、減低的
After being defeated for weeks, the moral of the troops have been degenerated .

在連續幾個星期都被擊敗後，軍隊的士氣已經渙散。

delighted (adj.) 開心愉悅的
People at the ceremony were all delighted and they all gave the newlyweds their best wishes.

在典禮上的人都十分開心而且都給予新婚夫婦最佳祝福。

問題 030 解答 (A) tweak 稍微修正

解答 他們需要**稍微修正**他們的商業模式才能興隆發達。

選項 (A) 稍微修正　(B) 阻塞　(C) 強調

補充例句

clog (v.) 阻塞
The doctor points out that too much cholesterol might clog up a patient's arteries.

醫生指出太多的膽固醇會阻塞病人的動脈。

highlight (v.) 強調
Dr. Johnson's speech highlighted the need for reforms.

強生博士的演講強調改革的需要。

The team has to come up with something to
_____ this problem before it gets to another
level.

   (A) upturn

   (B) conflict

   (C) counteract

A lot of experts and educators has formed a
committee to _____ the city's educational
options.

   (A) monitor

   (B) strive

   (C) canvass

解答 這個工作組必須在這個問題更嚴重之前，找出**應付**的方法。

選項 (A) 反轉　(B) 衝突　(C) 面對、應付

補充例句

upturn (v.) 反轉
No one has expected that the sales would upturn after a year in the bottom.

沒有人預期到銷售量會在谷底一年後反轉。

conflict (v.) 衝突
My work shift tomorrow conflicts with my class, can you help me wiggle it out?

我明天的工作排班跟我的課有衝突，你可以幫我想想辦法嗎？

解答 很多專家與教育者已組成了委員會來**遊說**這個城市的教育選擇權。

選項 (A) 監控　(B) 努力爭取　(C) 遊說

補充例句

monitor (v.) 監控
The CIA agent has monitored the Russian female spy's phone calls for few months.

中情局幹員已經監控這個蘇俄女間諜的電話好幾個月了。

strive (v.) 努力爭取
The boss wants everybody to strive for greater efficiency.

老闆要每個人努力爭取更好的效率。

問題 033

The government _____ the construction work of its subway, and one condition is that the contractor will be under its supervision.

(A) outsourced

(B) assigned

(C) shattered

問題 034

The new regulations require a reduction in harmful _____ from all the pharmaceutical companies.

(A) emissions

(B) debris

(C) showcases

問題 033 解答 (A) outsourced 外包

解答 政府將地鐵的興建工程**外包**出去，而且條件之一是要在政府的監督下。

選項 (A) 外包 (B) 指派 (C) 粉碎

補充例句

assigned (assign) (v.) 指派

The teacher left early without assigning homework.

老師在沒有交代功課的狀況下提早離開了。

shattered (shatter) (v.) 粉碎

The rumors about those innocent people should be shattered.

關於那些無辜人的謠言應該被粉碎。

問題 034 解答 (A) emissions 排放氣體

解答 新的政策要求所有藥廠減低有毒氣體的**排放**。

選項 (A) 排放氣體 (B) 殘骸 (C) 展示櫃

補充例句

debris (n.) 殘骸

It was sad to discover debris from the aircraft was scattered everywhere in the mountain.

發現飛機的殘骸在山中散落一地很令人難過。

showcase (n.) 展示櫃

The gallery provides a superior showcase for the artist's collections.

這間畫廊提供了一個很棒的展示櫃來放這個藝術家的收藏品。

Since their attitude is kind of _____ and fishy, I think that we need to have a backup plan.

(A) equivalent

(B) equivocal

(C) evident

In some rural area in the mountain, there is no supply of _____ water available.

(A) portable

(B) boastful

(C) potable

問題 035 解答 (B) equivocal 模稜兩可

解答 由於他們的態度有點**模稜兩可**而且值得懷疑，我認為我們需要有備用的計畫。

選項 (A) 相等的、相當的 (B) 模稜兩可 (C) 明顯的

補充例句

equivalent (adj.) 相等的、相當的
Tom's ability in math is equivalent to mine in art.
湯姆在數學上的能力和我在藝術上的能力相當。

evident (adj.) 明顯的
It's evident that Mike falls in love with her.
很明顯地，麥克愛上她了。

問題 036 解答 (C) potable 可直接飲用的

解答 在某些偏僻的山中，沒有供應可**直接飲用**的水。

選項 (A) 可攜帶的 (B) 吹牛的 (C) 可直接飲用的

補充例句

portable (adj.) 可攜帶的
A portable laptop computer is very useful for a salesperson.
對於一個業務員而言，可攜帶式的手提電腦是非常有用的。

boastful (adj.) 吹牛的
Psychologists think that a boastful person has a lot of insecurities.
心理學家認為一個愛吹牛的人本身很沒有安全感。

問題 037

Providing a relaxing and easy environment will definitely be _____ to the harmony of the whole work group.

(A) comprehensive

(B) tedious

(C) conducive

問題 038

It's hard to _____ how the employees will react when they hear the news.

(A) gauge

(B) garnish

(C) gaze

問題 037 解答 (C) conducive 有助益的

解答 建構一個放鬆的環境一定對整個工作組的和諧**有助益**。

選項 (A) 廣泛的　(B) 冗長的、乏味的　(C) 有助益的

補充例句

comprehensive (adj.) 廣泛的
This journal features a comprehensive collection of language articles.

這份期刊特色在於它廣泛蒐集語言相關的文章。

tedious (adj.) 冗長的、乏味的
Both students and guests were bored when listening to the tedious speech from the principle.

聆聽校長冗長而乏味的演講時，學生和來賓都感到無聊。

問題 038 解答 (A) gauge 評估

解答 很難**評估**員工聽到這個消息時會有什麼樣的反應。

選項 (A) 評估　(B) 裝飾　(C) 凝視

補充例句

garnish (v.) 裝飾
The salmon is garnished with baby corns and tiny carrots.

這道鮭魚以玉米筍和小紅蘿蔔做裝飾。

gaze (v.) 凝視
The manager doesn't want to work so he simply gazes out of the window.

經理不想工作所以他僅是凝視著窗外。

問題 039

People need to be _____ during this typhoon season especially the residents living in low-lying areas.

      (A) assessed

      (B) alerted

      (C) authorized

問題 040

The aborigines need education and more economic opportunities in order to _____ themselves from poverty.

      (A) extricate

      (B) extradite

      (C) exterminate

解答 在颱風季節期間，人們必須被**警告**，尤其是居住在低窪地區的居民。

選項 (A) 評估、評價 (B) 警告、警示 (C) 授權

補充例句

assessed (adj.)(assess)(v.) 評估、評價
The school has been working on a program to assess the students' English ability.

學校目前在運作一個方案來評估學生的英文能力。

authorized (adj.) (authorize)(v.) 授權
Only authorized people are allowed to enter this area.

只有經過授權的人才被允許進入這個區域。

解答 原住民需要教育與更多的經濟機會讓他們能夠**脫離貧困**。

選項 (A) 脫困 (B) 引渡 (C) 消滅

補充例句

extradite (v.) 引渡
The fraudster was caught by the Japanese police and extradited to Taiwan.

這個詐欺犯被日本警方逮捕並被引渡回台灣。

exterminate (v.) 消滅
Countless Jewish people were exterminated in concentration camps in WWII.

二次大戰時無以計數的猶太人在集中營中被消滅。

Our thirty-year old bungalow, after being
_____ , looks new and stylish.

(A) refurbished

(B) generated

(C) reinforced

The _____ of this small island include
earthquakes, typhoons, landslides and floods.

(A) hazards

(B) hallmarks

(C) hazes

問題 041 解答 (A) refurbished 重新裝潢整理

解答 我們三十年的老房子在**重新裝潢**後看起來又新穎又具風格。

選項 (A) 重新裝潢整理　(B) 衍生、引起　(C) 加強

補充例句

generated (generate) (v.) 衍生、引起
We need to generate more and better ideas for our new campaign.

我們需要為新的選舉戰想出更多更好的點子來。

reinforced (reinforce) (v.) 加強
You need to reinforce your vocabulary capacity if you want to master English.

如果你想要掌握好英文,就必須加強你的字彙量。

問題 042 解答 (A) hazards 危險

解答 這個小島的**危險**源包含地震、颱風、土石流與水災。

選項 (A) 危險　(B) 特徵　(C) 薄霧

補充例句

hallmark (n.) 特徵
The architect believes simplicity is the hallmark of all designs.

這個建築師相信簡單就是所有設計的特徵。

haze (n.) 薄霧
The solider saw the lieutenant through a haze of smoke.

這個士兵從香菸的薄霧中看見了中尉。

You can easily find there's a _____
development in this project and we will surely
see its success.

(A) subsequent

(B) suspicious

(C) sustainable

Mr. Johnson has been here for a long time so he
is _____ to apply for citizenship.

(A) equipped

(B) exposed

(C) entitled

解答 你可以輕易發現在這個方案上有**持續性的**發展,而我們必會看到它成功。

選項 (A) 後來的　(B) 懷疑的　(C) 有持續性的、具支撐的

補充例句

subsequent (adj.) 後來的

In subsequent years, traveling became the most important part of her life.

在接下來的幾年裡,旅遊變成她生活當中最重要的部分。

suspicious (adj.) 懷疑的

Being a suspicious person, Ms. Johnson trusts no one.

作為一個疑心病重的人,強森女士不相信任何人。

解答 強納生先生在這裡已經很久了,所以他有**資格**申請成為公民。

選項 (A) 賦予　(B) 暴露　(C) 資格

補充例句

equip (v.) 賦予

Martha's degree in business administration actually equips her for many jobs.

瑪莎的商業管理學位實際上讓她許多工作的資格。

expose (v.) 暴露

Humans bodies need to be exposed to sunlight in order to make vitamin D.

人體需要暴露在陽光底下才能獲取維他命 D。

Though it's considered cruel, animal testing is
_____ to medical field.

(A) incredible

(B) essential

(C) vulnerable

Our secretary, Anna, is of a cheerful and sunny
_____.

(A) delegate

(B) deregulation

(C) disposition

問題 045 解答 (B) essential 不可或缺的

解答 動物實驗對於藥物界是**不可或缺的**，儘管這被認為很
殘忍。

選項 (A) 不可思議的　(B) 不可或缺的　(C) 脆弱的

補充例句

incredible (adj.) 開明的
The July 4th fireworks at Macy's were incredibly beautiful and
it actually attracted people from around New York city to come
and watch.
**七月四日梅西百貨的煙火真是非常美麗，事實上它吸引了紐約市很
多人前來觀看。**

vulnerable (adj.) 脆弱的
He's still vulnerable after the surgery. Please take good care of
him.
他在手術後還是很虛弱，請你好好照顧他。

問題 046 解答 (C) disposition 性情

解答 我們的祕書安娜有愉悅而開朗的**性情**。

選項 (A) 代表　(B) 撤銷規定　(C) 性情

補充例句

delegate (n.) 代表
Each state needs to choose several delegates to the national
convention.
每一州都需要選幾個代表參加國家會議。

deregulation (n.) 撤銷管制規定
Some experts are worried about that the deregulation of
broadcasting might lead to a lowering of standards.
有些專家擔心廣播限制的放寬，將會導致廣播標準的降低。

My meat-loving brother can't stand listening to me _____ the virtues of a vegetarian diet.

      (A) extolling

      (B) persuading

      (C) pursuing

Nobody has been living in this log cabin for the past ten years so it needs a lot of _____ .

      (A) maintenance

      (B) ambivalence

      (C) essence

問題 047 解答 (A) extolling 讚揚

解答 我那愛吃肉的哥哥無法忍受聽我**讚揚**素食的好處。

選項 (A) 讚揚 (B) 說服 (C) 追求

補充例句

persuade (v.) 說服
There's no use persuading your stubborn father. I bet he'll never agree with your idea of working abroad.

不可能說服你頑固的老爸的。我敢說他不會同意你出國工作的念頭。

persue (v.) 追求
We all want to be pursued by good luck and opportunities.

我們都想要有好運和機會跟隨。

問題 048 解答 (A) maintenance 維修

解答 過去十年沒人住這間小木屋，所以它需要**修繕**的地方很多。

選項 (A) 維修 (B) 矛盾 (C) 本質

補充例句

ambivalence (n.) 矛盾
I feel that my ambivalence is increasing over time.

我覺得我的矛盾心理隨著時間一直在增長。

essence (n.) 本質
The essence of her argument is that we should take good care of our companion animals.

她的基本論點是我們需要好好照顧陪伴我們的動物。

After reviewing that investment scheme, I'm pretty sure that it must be a _____ because the expected profit is unbelievable high.

       (A) bribery

       (B) blackmail

       (C) scam

The female applicant is quite reserved but the male applicant tends to be _____.

       (A) effusive

       (B) exclusive

       (C) extensive

問題 049 解答 (C) scam 欺詐騙局

解答 在審視過這個投資方案後，我很確信這一定是**詐欺**，
因為它的預期獲利是難以置信的高。

選項 (A) 賄賂 (B) 敲詐勒索 (C) 欺詐、騙局

補充例句

bribery (n.) 賄賂
Tom got his position in this company through an act of bribery.

湯姆用賄賂的手段得到他在公司的職位。

blackmail (v.) 敲詐勒索
Becky's ex-boyfriend's been blackmailing and threatening her.

貝琪的前男友一直在威脅勒索她。

問題 050 解答 (A) effusive 太熱情的

解答 這位女性應徵者相當保守，但這位男性應徵者則趨向
於**過度熱情**。

選項 (A) 太熱情的 (B) 唯一的 (C) 廣泛的

補充例句

exclusive (adj.) 唯一的
This gym is for the exclusive use of guests.

這間健身房是專門給嘉賓使用的。

extensive (adj.) 廣泛的
The hurricane caused extensive damage in this area.

颶風對這個區域造成了很大的災害。

問題 051

The board of directors is still looking for someone _____ to run the company.

(A) mutual

(B) eligible

(C) thrifty

問題 052

The director has been _____ from his job for incompetence.

(A) declined

(B) facilitated

(C) dismissed

解答 董事會仍然在找尋一位**合適的**人選來經營公司。

選項 (A) 互相的　(B) 合適的　(C) 節儉的

補充例句

mutual (adj.) 互相的
To form a good relationship, mutual trust is the key.
營造一個好的關係，互相的信任是其關鍵。

thrifty (adj.) 節儉的
My sister is a thrifty and pragmatic shopper and she also knows how to bargain.
我妹妹是個節約且務實的購物者，而且她真的知道如何殺價。

解答 由於無能，這位局長已經被**卸除職務**了。

選項 (A) 拒絕　(B) 協助　(C) 卸除職務

補充例句

decline (v.) 拒絕
The new couple declined to be interviewed by the media.
這對新婚夫婦拒絕所有媒體的訪問。

facilitate (v.) 協助
There are a lot of ways to facilitate this plan going forward so don't worry about it.
有很多方式可以協助這個計畫進行，所以不用擔心。

Leanne never keeps up with any work schedule and she often _____ . Her annual report is late for almost one month.

(A) prevails

(B) procrastinates

(C) ponders

Traffic will be _____ through Park Road while the road is resurfaced.

(A) retreated

(B) adapted

(C) diverted

問題 053 解答　(B) procrastinate 拖延

解答　莉安從來都跟不上任何工作進度而且總是**拖延**。她的年度報告就遲了幾乎一個月。

選項　(A) 勝過、流行　(B) 拖延　(C) 考慮、沈思

補充例句

prevail (v.) 勝過、流行
Some people do believe that good will always prevails evil.
有些人真的相信好心總是戰勝邪惡。

ponder (v.) 考慮、沈思
He pondered over my questions for a considerable time before coming up with an answer.
他針對我的問題先沈思了好一會兒才回答。

問題 054 解答　(C) diverted 改道

解答　當這一條路重新鋪路面時，交通會**改道**到公園路上。

選項　(A) 撤退　(B) 適應　(C) 改道

補充例句

retreat (v.) 撤退
The helicopter was forced to retreat back because of the sever snowstorm so the rescue plan failed.
直昇機在嚴重的暴風雪中被迫撤退，所以救援計畫失敗了。

adapt (v.) 適應
The new hire tries hard to adapt herself to the new environment.
那位新手很努力地嘗試去適應新的環境。

114

Working day and night on this project really
_____ my energy. I'll definitely get a
vacation after it's completed.

(A) dried

(B) induced

(C) drained

Microsoft is _____ to launch its new
advertising campaign.

(A) poised

(B) diverse

(C) decisive

問題 055 解答 (C) drained 用盡

解答 不分晝夜地執行這個案子讓我**筋疲力盡**。在它完成後我一定要休個長假。

選項 (A) 弄乾 (B) 引用 (C) 用盡

補充例句

dried (dry) (v.) 弄乾
You can use that towel to dry your hands after you wash them.
你可以在洗手後用那條毛巾擦乾。

induce (v.) 引誘
Helen is a successful realtor because she knows how to induce customers to buy houses.
海倫是位成功的房地產經紀人，因為她知道如何勸誘客戶買房子。

問題 056 解答 (A) poised 蓄勢待發的

解答 微軟**準備好**開始它新的廣告活動。

選項 (A) 蓄勢待發的 (B) 多樣的 (C) 有決斷力的

補充例句

diverse (adj.) 多樣的
Taipei is a very diverse city with a rich culture and history.
台北是一個非常多樣化的城市，擁有豐富的文化與歷史。

decisive (adj.) 有決斷的
I am not sure if he will give a decisive answer.
我不確定他是否會給出一個堅決的答案。

問題 057

The doctor told me not to drive after taking this medicine because it may make you _____.

      (A) drenched

      (B) envious

      (C) drowsy

問題 058

If human beings continue to _____ the earth's natural resources, the world will be destroyed soon.

      (A) aggregate

      (B) resolve

      (C) deplete

解答 醫生告訴我吃完這藥後不要開車，因為這個藥會讓你**頭昏**。

選項 (A) 濕透的　(B) 羨慕的　(C) 昏沈的

補充例句

drench (adj.) 濕透的
We were all drenched after playing four hours of basketball outside.

在戶外打了四個小時籃球之後，我們全身都濕透了。

envious (adj.) 羨慕的
My little sister is so envious when she sees us go to school and make friends.

我的小妹看到我們去上學校，還了交朋友，好生羨慕。

解答 如果人類繼續**耗盡**地球的天然資源，世界將會很快被摧毀。

選項 (A) 聚集　(B) 決心　(C) 耗盡

補充例句

aggregate (v.) 聚集
The fans aggregated ten thousand people in an hour.

粉絲們在一小時內聚集了一萬人。

resolve (v.) 決心
The new director resolves to expand the business all over the world.

新的執行長決心要將業務擴展到全世界。

問題 059

After I arrive at New York, my co-worker there will meet me at the airport and take me to the

_____ .

(A) reservation

(B) residence

(C) accommodation

問題 060

Jenny didn't want her colleagues to think that she was _____ for a promotion.

(A) conjuring

(B) angling

(C) releasing

問題 059 解答 (C)accommodation 住宿所 (短期)

解答 我抵達紐約後，當地同事會在機場與我碰面，帶我去**住所**。

選項 (A) 預約 (B) 居所 (C) 住宿所 (短期)

補充例句

reservation (n.) 預約
That restaurant is really popular. You won't get a table if you don't have a reservation in advance.

那間餐廳真的很受歡迎。如果你不預先訂位，是不會有位子的。

residence (n.) 居所
Besides their house in Taipei city, they have a summer residence in Australia.

他們除了台北市的房子外，在澳洲也有一間避暑的住宅。

問題 060 解答 (B) angling 設法博取

解答 珍妮不想要讓她的同事認為她**設法獲得**升遷。

選項 (A) 讓人聯想 (B) 設法博取 (C) 釋放

補充例句

conjure (v.) 讓人聯想
This playground conjures up vivid memories.

這個操場讓人聯想到清晰生動的往事。

release (v.) 釋放、發行
The terrorists had released two of the hostages.

恐怖份子已經釋放了其中兩個人質。

問題 061

Since he got _____ in politics, he rarely has time for his family.

        (A) endorsed

        (B) engaged

        (C) expired

問題 062

The government is planning to _____ the postal service and the rail services.

        (A) coordinate

        (B) appreciate

        (C) privatize

問題 061 解答 (B) engaged 涉入、吸引、訂婚

解答　自從他**涉入**政治以後，他鮮少有時間陪家人。

選項　(A) 背書　(B) 涉入、吸引、訂婚　(C) 到期

補充例句

endorsed (endorse) (v.) 背書
I really need you to endorse my new product. People will definitely buy it if it's endorsed by a celebrity.

我真的需要你幫我的產品背書，如果有名人背書，大家一定會買的。

expired (expire) (v.) 到期
Go and finish up the milk before it expires.

在牛奶過期之前去把它喝完。

問題 062 解答 (C) privatize 私有化、民營化

解答　政府正計畫把郵政及鐵路服務**民營化**。

選項　(A) 協調　(B) 感激　(C) 私有化、民營化

補充例句

coordinate (v.) 協調
The marketing director coordinates the marketing campaign.

這位行銷總監協調所有行銷活動。

appreciate (v.) 感激
Thank you for backing me up. I really appreciate it.

非常感謝你支持我，我真的很感激。

問題 063

The whole class is going to have a(an) _____ to the lab at the medical center this afternoon.

(A) excursion

(B) remainder

(C) illuminate

問題 064

John liked Japan a lot because the local people showed him great _____ .

(A) capacity

(B) authority

(C) hospitality

問題 063 解答 (A) excursion 短程旅遊或參訪

解答 今天下午全班要去醫學中心的實驗室**參訪**。

選項 (A) 短程旅遊或參訪 (B) 其餘的人 (C) 照亮、照射

補充例句

remainder (n.) 餘下的人
Please tell the remainders to wait in the conference room during the recession.

請告訴餘下的人在休息期間到會議室裡等候。

illuminate (v.) 照亮、照射
This room was too dark after sunset, so we have to turn on the light to illuminate it.

這個房間在太陽下山後變得很暗，所以我們必須開燈讓它亮起來。

問題 064 解答 (C) hospitality 熱情

解答 約翰很喜歡日本，因為當地人對他很**熱情**。

選項 (A) 容量 (B) 當局 (C) 熱情

補充例句

capacity (n.) 容量
The stadium has a seating capacity of 10,000.

這座體育場可以容納一萬個人。

authority (n.) 當局
The authorities in Canada have refused to allow her to enter the country.

加拿大當局已經拒絕讓她進入這個國家。

問題 065

In my country, the _____ of the president is four years. In other words, there's a presidential election every four years.

(A) contraption

(B) tenure

(C) pledge

問題 066

The hypermarket promises that all members get the price benefit of _____ buying.

(A) fiscal

(B) dire

(C) bulk

問題 065 解答　(B) tenure 任期

解答　在我的國家，總統**任期**是四年。也就是說，每四年就有一次總統選舉。

選項　(A) 新奇的機械或發明　(B) 任期　(C) 保證

補充例句

contraption (n.)　新奇的機械或發明
I went to the computer show at the world trade center and found some creative contraptions.

我去了世貿的電腦展，看到了一些有創意的新發明。

pledge (n.)　保證
In recent years, graduation pledge which was started from our school has become quite popular.

近幾年來，從我們學校開始的畢業生宣言變得很受歡迎。

問題 066 解答　(C) bulk 大量的

解答　這間大賣場承諾所有會員都可享有**大宗**買賣的優惠價。

選項　(A) 會計的、財政的　(B) 悲慘的、嚴重的　(C) 大量的

補充例句

fiscal (adj.)　財政的、會計的
The government is making new fiscal and monetary policies.

政府正在制訂新的財政與貨幣政策。

dire (adj.)　悲慘的、嚴重的
Iceland has faced financial crisis so the country is in dire straits.

冰島已面臨財政危機，所以這個國家正處於極端困難的境地。

問題 067

When Samuel was still a(an) _____
actor, once he almost decided to give up and
fortunately he met his agent who restored his
faith.

(A) tricky

(B) alert

(C) struggling

問題 068

In a _____ attempt to escape from the
building, the suspect shot two guards.

(A) considerate

(B) desperate

(C) moderate

問題 067 解答 (C) struggling 奮鬥掙扎的

解答 當山姆還在星途中**努力**時，他曾幾乎想要放棄，但幸運地碰到了幫助他重拾信心的經紀人。

選項 (A) 難辨的、狡猾的 (B) 留心的 (C) 奮鬥掙扎的

補充例句

tricky (adj.) 難辨的、狡猾的
You sounded tricky. I can sense there's something between lines here.

你聽起來有點詭異哦！我覺得你話中有話。

alert (adj.) 留心的
I'd like you to stay alert while you're on duty.

我希望你在當班時保持警覺。

問題 068 解答 (B) desperate 拼命的

解答 嫌犯在**拼命地**嘗試從大樓逃跑時，對兩名警衛開槍。

選項 (A) 體貼的 (B) 拼命的 (C) 適度的

補充例句

considerate (adj.) 體貼的
It was very considerate of you to invite me.

你真體貼，邀請我來。

moderate (adj.) 適度的
The tone of her speech was quite moderate.

她演講的語調相當溫和。

問題 069

In this ecological reserve, we can see some protected animals and a few _____ animals.

        (A) extinct

        (B) endangered

        (C) tortured

問題 070

The NGO is _____ for stricter laws to control toxic waste from the pharmaceutical companies.

        (A) lobbying

        (B) resuming

        (C) defying

問題 069 解答 (B) endangered 瀕臨絕種的

解答　在這個生態保育區，我們可看到一些保育類動物，和少數**瀕臨絕種**的動物。

選項　(A) 絕種的　(B) 瀕臨絕種的　(C) 保育的、受保護的

補充例句

extinct (adj.) 絕種的
Scientists are doing experiments to revive ancient extinct animals such as dinosaurs.

科學家在進行實驗，讓絕種的遠古動物譬如恐龍復活。

tortureded (adj.) 受折磨的
Not all animals on earth are protected. Just yesterday, on the news, we saw a new born baby dog was tortured to death by a little boy.

地球上並非所有動物都被保護。昨晚，新聞上就看到了一隻新生狗兒被小男孩折磨至死。

問題 070 解答 (A) lobbying 遊說

解答　這個非政府組織**遊說**訂立更嚴苛的法條，以控制製藥公司排出的有毒廢物。

選項　(A) 遊說　(B) 重新開始　(C) 公然反抗

補充例句

resume (v.) 重新開始
We will stop now and resume our discussions in the afternoon.

我們現在先暫停，下午再重新開始討論。

defy (v.) 公然反抗
The candidate defied his party leader and decided to launch his election campaign.

這個候選人公然反抗黨的領導者，並且決定開始他的選舉活動。

Though it seems easy for J. K. Rowling to become the most _____ writer, she claims that there was a downtime for her too.

(A) unattached

(B) resolute

(C) resilient

The dollar has _____ to records lows against RMB.

(A) trebled

(B) soared

(C) slumped

問題 071 解答 (C) resilient 具市場活力的

解答　雖然 J. K. 羅琳看來輕易地成為一個**有適應力的**作家，她表示也曾經過一段人生的谷底。

選項　(A) 無所屬的　(B) 堅決的　(C) 有適應力的

補充例句

unattached (adj.) 不受約束的
It's better that we stay unattached.

我們最好還是保持距離，不相往來。

resolute (v.) resolution (n) 決心
What's your New Year's resolution? I suggest that you can make quitting smoking the number one of them.

妳的新年新希望是什麼？我建議你可以把戒菸列為所有新希望的第一項。

問題 072 解答 (C) slumped 暴跌

解答　美元對人民幣已經創了歷史新低。

選項　(A) 成長三倍　(B) 飆升　(C) 暴跌

補充例句

treble (v.) 成長三倍
Oil prices have more than trebled since January.

油價從一月起已經成長超過三倍。

soar (v.) 飆升
House prices have soared to an all-time high in Taipei.

台北的房價已經升到歷史新高。

Since the company is still on its way back from the _____ , we do need to keep our fingers crossed that the market strategies will work.

(A) stagnation

(B) clientele

(C) barricade

We all know that bad weather means fruit and vegetable prices are set to _____ .

(A) rocket

(B) plummet

(C) plunge

解答　既然公司仍然在從**不景氣**中恢復的路上，我們真的需要
　　　人人祈求我們的市場策略奏效。

選項　(A) 不景氣　(B) 客戶群　(C) 路障

補充例句

clientele (n.) 客戶群
Doris knows there's a wealthy clientele for this particular stone of art.

陶樂斯知道這種特別的石頭藝術有一群富有的客戶群。

barricade (n.) 路障
The protest crowds became so aggressive that the police had to set up barricades at the front gates.

抗議群眾變得非常激進，警察不得不在大門上設置路障。

解答　我們都知道壞天氣就表示水果與蔬菜價格會**暴漲**。

選項　(A) 激增　(B) 驟降　(C) 暴跌

補充例句

plummet (v.) 驟降
The president's popularity rating has plummeted in recent months.

總統的支持率在最近幾個月已經驟降。

plunge (v.) 暴跌
The price of gold has plunged to a new low.

黃金的價格已經降到新低了。

The hardest part for junior high teachers is to
_____ the students. Even the ones with
good grades may have problematic behaviors.

        (A) discern

        (B) discipline

        (C) discover

The bank was threatening to _____ on
Molly's mortgage because she failed to keep up
her mortgage payments.

        (A) foresee

        (B) foreclose

        (C) forecast

問題 075 解答 (B) discipline 規範、使有紀律

解答　國中老師工作中最難的部分在於**規範**學生。即使成績好的學生也可能有偏差行為。

選項　(A) 分辨、辨識　(B) 規範、使有紀律　(C) 發現

補充例句

discern (v.) 分辨、辨識
School teachers are reinforcing the clear ideas of students to know how to discern right from wrong.

學校老師正在加強學生清楚的概念，知道如何分辨對錯。

discover (v.) 發現
The research team finally discovered some equipment left by the victims, so they believed that there must be a chance to rescue them.
這個探索小組終於發現遇難者留下的一些設備，因此相信一定有機以營救他們。

問題 076 解答 (B) foreclose 取消贖回權

解答　銀行威脅要取消茉莉的**贖回權**，因為她沒有按時繳交她的房屋貸款。

選項　(A) 預見　(B) 取消贖回權　(C) 預報

補充例句

foresee (v.) 預見
It's impossible to foresee such problems.
要預見這樣的問題是不可能的。

forecast (n.) 預報
The weather forecast on TV said there would be afternoon showers in the north.
電視的氣象預報說今天北部會有午後雷陣雨。

問題 077

Whenever we get stocked with some projects or issues, my supervisor would have us all sit down and _____ .

        (A) brainchild

        (B) brainstorm

        (C) brainpower

問題 078

We want to buy an apartment, _____ they would rather rent one.

        (A) whereas

        (B) whenever

        (C) whether

問題 077 解答　(B) brainstorm 集思廣益

解答　每當我們在一個案子或提議中碰到瓶頸，我的主管就會
叫我們大家坐下來**集思廣益**。

選項　(A) 獨創概念　(B) 集思廣益　(C) 腦力

補充例句

brainchild (n.) 獨創概念

Having staff work from home to save rent and cut costs is the
brainchild of our marketing manager.

讓員工在家工作以節省房租和成本，是我們行銷經理的創意想法。

brainpower (n.) 腦力

Some people believe that brainpower can actually help people
achieve certain goals.

有些人相信腦力事實上可以幫助人達成一定的目標。

問題 078 解答　(A) whereas 然而

解答　我們想要買一間公寓，**然而**他們卻寧願租一間。

選項　(A) 然而　(B) 每當　(C) 是否

補充例句

whenever (conj.) 每當

Whenever I hear that song, I can't help feeling sad.

每當我聽到那首歌，我就忍不住覺得傷心。

whether (conj.) 是否

We don't know whether she is coming to the meeting or not.

我們不知道她是否要來參加會議。

Grandmother gave me the ring for my wedding. She said it was _____ in both price and family tradition.

(A) inevitable

(B) invasive

(C) invaluable

I'm afraid I can't join you because I'm attending my best friend's wedding _____.

(A) bouquet

(B) boutique

(C) banquet

解答 祖母為了我的婚禮送給我鑽戒。她說這個鑽戒不論在
價錢上或家庭傳統而言都**非常貴重**。

選項 (A) 無法避免的 (B) 侵略的 (C) 非常貴重的

補充例句

inevitable (adj.) 無法避免的
Even doctors would say that it's kind of inevitable for
teenagers to be rebellious.

連醫生都說青少年有點叛逆是無可避免的。

invasive (adj.) 侵略的
One of the key tasks of the UN is to stop any invasive wars
from happening.

聯合國的主要任務之一是阻止任何侵略戰爭發生。

解答 我恐怕無法加入你們了，因為我要參加我最好朋友
的**喜宴**。

選項 (A) 花束 (B) 精品店 (C) 宴會

補充例句

bouquet (n.) 花束
He gave her a bouquet of red roses and proposed to her.

他送她一束紅玫瑰並向她求婚。

boutique (n.) 精品店
There are many boutiques along the street.

這條街沿路有很多精品店。

問題 081

Showing _____ to the elders is something that should be emphasized to all young people.

(A) reverberation

(B) reverie

(C) reverence

問題 082

All soldiers _____ allegiance to the constitution of the U.S..

(A) swindled

(B) sweated

(C) swore

問題 081 解答 (C) reverence 尊敬

解答 對長者表示**尊重**和敬意應該是要向年輕人強調的事。

選項 (A) 影響、回響 (B) 白日夢、幻想曲 (C) 尊敬

補充例句

reverberation (n.) 影響、回響
The family violence had a lot of reverberations on his misconduct.

家庭暴力對於他的不良行為有很大的影響。

reverie (n.) 白日夢、（音樂）幻想曲
I hate to break you from your reverie, but it's the final stop and you need to get off.

我很抱歉要打擾你的白日夢，不過這裡是終點站，你必須下車了。

問題 082 解答 (C) swore 宣誓

解答 所有的士兵都必須**宣誓**效忠美國憲法。

選項 (A) 詐騙 (B) 流汗 (C) 宣誓

補充例句

swindle (v.) 詐騙
The bank clerk was accused of swindling millions of dollars out of several clients.

銀行行員被控從許多客戶帳戶內詐取數百萬元。

sweat (v.) 流汗
I am so nervous that I feel the palms of my hands sweating.

我好緊張所以我感覺到我的手掌在冒汗。

Thousands of workers are protesting for a(an) _____ to the current but out-dated labor law.

(A) amendment

(B) exploration

(C) compensation

The motivational speaker stood behind the _____ and was welcomed by a crowd of 20,000.

(A) kiosk

(B) stadium

(C) podium

問題 083 解答 (A) amendment 改正、修定

解答 上千名勞工抗議要求針對目前過時的勞工法做**修正**。

選項 (A) 改正、修定 (B) 探查、瞭解 (C) 補償金、賠償

補充例句

exploration (n.) 探查、瞭解
Experts suggest that parents should provide children opportunities of exploration the world.

專家建議父母應該要提供孩子更多機會去探索世界。

compensation (n.) 補償金、賠償
A visitor who got neck injured received reasonable compensation.

一個脖子受傷的遊客，得到了合理的賠償。

問題 084 解答 (C) podium 講台

解答 這位有感染力的演說家站在**講台**後並受到兩萬人的歡迎。

選項 (A) 小攤子 (B) 體育場 (C) 講台

補充例句

kiosk (n.) 小攤子
You can buy newspapers and magazines from the kiosk on the corner.

你可以在轉角的小攤子買報紙與雜誌。

stadium (n.) 體育場
The stadium can accommodate up to 20,000 people.

這個體育場可以容納兩萬人。

問題 085

Every job has its _____ . Once you can manage it well, you'll find it easy to work efficiently and effectively.

(A) funds

(B) functions

(C) fundamentals

問題 086

Although Jason's family is extremely wealthy, they were never _____ .

(A) inauspicious

(B) ostentatious

(C) superstitious

解答　每份工作都有它的**基本綱領**與原則。只要你可以掌握它，你將發現迅速有效率的工作是容易的。

選項　(A) 基金　(B) 功能　(C) 基本綱要

補充例句

fund (n.) 基金
My father has saved my education fund, so we don't need to worry if I want to go to college.

我父親把我的教育基金存好了，所以如果我要念大學也不用擔心。

function (n.) 功能
Can you demonstrate how to use this all-in-1 service machine? We are still not familiar with its functions.

你能教我如何使用這台全功能的事務機？我們還是不熟悉其功能。

解答　雖然傑森的家裡相當有錢，但是他們從來不擺闊。

選項　(A) 不吉祥的　(B) 浮誇的　(C) 迷信的

補充例句

inauspicious (adj.) 不吉祥的
The baseball player made an inauspicious start by twisting his shoulder in the game.

這個棒球選手在比賽中扭傷了肩膀，真是一個不吉祥的開始。

superstitious (adj.) 迷信的
It's not surprising to know that a lot of athletes are rather superstitious.

有很多運動員相當迷信，這一點都不令人驚訝。

146

In order to _____ the operation, the manager proposed that workers should be in three shifts.

      (A) strive

      (B) struggle

      (C) streamline

We have tried in vain so it's time to _____ idealism with reality.

      (A) vanish

      (B) recover

      (C) temper

問題 087 解答 (C) streamline 使更有效率

解答 為了工作**更有效率**，這位經理建議把員工分成三班。

選項 (A) 努力達到　(B) 掙扎　(C) 使更有效率

補充例句

strive (v.) 努力達到
Though people kept on ignoring him, he still strove to make himself noticed.

雖然大家一直忽略他，他還是努力地要讓自己被注意到。

struggle (v.) 掙扎
Since he's not doing well in this industry, he struggles whether he should give up on all his prior endeavors.

因為他在這行做得並不好，他掙扎著是否要放棄之前所有的努力。

問題 088 解答 (C) temper 緩和

解答 我們嘗試過但失敗，所以是時候將理想與現實**調和**了。

選項 (A) 消失　(B) 回復　(C) 緩和

補充例句

vanish (v.) 消失
The suspect vanished in to the darkness.

嫌犯消失在暗夜中。

recover (v.) 回復
The restaurant hopes to recover the cost of buying all the equipment two years.

餐廳希望兩年內能夠將買設備的費用回收。

問題 089

The government is trying to come up with a
_____ plan to save the insurance industry.

    (A) bailout

    (B) bond

    (C) backup

問題 090

The presidents of the U.S. calls for the economic
_____ package.

    (A) stimulus

    (B) ambiguous

    (C) conscious

問題 089 解答　(A) bailout 紓困、援助

解答　政府正在嘗試找出一個**紓困**方案來解救保險業。

選項　(A) 紓困、援助　(B) 連結　(C) 補救、備案

補充例句

bond (n.) 連結
We've been best friends for over thirty years, so we both sense there's a special bond between us.

我們是三十多年的朋友了，所以我們覺得彼此有一種特殊的聯繫。

backup (adj.) 補救、備案
Do you have any backup plans just in case there are any unexpected situations?

如果有任何意外狀況發生，你有補救的計畫嗎？

問題 090 解答　(A) stimulus 激發、刺激

解答　美國總統呼籲支持經濟復甦方案。

選項　(A) 激發、刺激　(B) 模糊不清的　(C) 知覺的

補充例句

ambiguous (adj.) 曖昧的、不明的
We can't do anything because the CEO has been ambiguous on this issue.

我們無法做任何事，因為總裁對這個議題一直都是模稜兩可的。

conscious (adj.) 知覺的
He is not conscious that someone is standing behind him for a long time.

他沒有察覺有人站在他後面好久一段時間。

Once he knew that Samuel has been spreading rumors about him, he can't conceal his _____ when he sees him.

        (A) hostility

        (B) permissiveness

        (C) absurdity

The problems had been solved _____ to his arrival.

        (A) besides

        (B) prior

        (C) furthermore

問題 091 解答　(A) hostility 敵意、敵視

解答 當他一知道山繆在散布關於他的謠言，他看到山繆時便無法控制對他的**敵意**。

選項 (A) 敵意、敵視　(B) 放任、放縱　(C) 荒誕行為

補充例句

permissiveness (n.) 放任、放縱
The permissiveness behaviors of the teenagers annoyed the other passengers.

這些青少年的放任行為惹惱了其他乘客。

absurdity (n.) 荒誕行為
Melissa appreciates the awareness of the absurdity of human existence in Samuel Beckett's work.

瑪莉莎很欣賞山繆爾貝克特作品裡對人類存在之荒謬的覺醒。

問題 092 解答　(B) prior 在…之前

解答 **在**他到達**前**問題已經被解決了。

選項 (A) 除了　(B) 在…之前　(C) 此外

補充例句

besides (prep.) 除了
Besides making money, he invests a lot of money in the stock market.

除了賺錢，他在股市中投資很多錢。

furthermore (prep.) 此外
The house is just right for a family of three, and furthermore, it is in a good location.

這間房子剛好適合三口之家，此外，它的位置相當棒。

問題 093

An _____ person frequently disagrees with what other people say.

        (A) obstinate

        (B) even-tempered

        (C) assertive

問題 094

The young singer is a _____ performer.

        (A) virtual

        (B) variable

        (C) versatile

問題 093 解答 (C) assertive 武斷的

解答 一個**武斷的**人經常不同意他人的說法。

選項 (A) 頑強、不屈服的 (B) 穩重的 (C) 武斷的

補充例句

obstinate (adj.) 頑強、不屈服的
He's so obstinate and every time we try to persuade him not to do something, he ends up becoming even more determined.
他真是非常固執。每當我們試圖去說服他不要做某件事時，他總是更堅決地去做。

even-tempered (adj.) 穩重的
I enjoy being with someone who's even-tempered because I don't want to deal with any sudden and unexpected angers or depressions.
我喜歡跟個性沈穩的人在一起，因為我不需要應付突如其來的憤怒或沮喪。

問題 094 解答 (C) versatile 多才多藝的

解答 這個年輕的歌手是一個**多才多藝**的表演者。

選項 (A) 虛擬的 (B) 變數 (C) 多才多藝的

補充例句

virtual (adj.) 虛擬的
There are virtual communities on the Internet.
網路上有虛擬的社區。

variable (n.) 變數
All these variables can affect the results of the research.
所有這些變數都會影響到研究的結果。

Patricia's been trying so many different ways to lose weight but she's still kind of _____ .

- (A) plump
- (B) obese
- (C) stocky

The motorcyclist is _____ for the cost of the car repairs.

- (A) distressed
- (B) queasy
- (C) liable

問題 095 解答 (A) plump 豐腴的、微胖的

解答 派翠莎嘗試了許多方法減重，但看起來仍然很**豐腴**。

選項 (A) 豐腴的、微胖的 (B) 肥胖的、過胖的 (C) 矮壯的

補充例句

obese (adj.) 肥胖的、過胖的
Our math teacher is in fact an obese person but he claims that he's only a little overweight.

我們數學老師真的很胖，但他宣稱自己只是有一點點過重。

stocky (adj.) 矮壯的
My father isn't tall but he's stocky. Compare with other men at his age, he's really in good shape.

我父親不高但很壯。跟他同年齡的人相比，他的體格算很好。

問題 096 解答 (C) liable 有償付責任

解答 這個騎士需要**負責**車子修理費用。

選項 (A) 煩惱的 (B) 反胃的 (C) 有償付責任的

補充例句

distressed (adj.) 煩惱的
He is distressed to find out that his partner hasn't come back.

他很煩惱，因為他發現他的夥件還沒有回來。

queasy (adj.) 反胃的
She felt a sudden queasy in the car when we were driving into the mountain road.

當我們開進山路時，她在車內突然有反胃的感覺。

Floods damaged most farmlands, millions of people will be suffering from _____ .

        (A) drought

        (B) famine

        (C) eruption

Many explanations for the serious plane crash were _____ in the media.

        (A) floated

        (B) retrieved

        (C) endorsed

問題 097 解答 (B) famine 饑荒

解答 洪水摧毀了大部分的農田，百萬人口將因為**饑荒**而受苦。

選項 (A) 乾旱 (B) 饑荒 (C) 爆發

補充例句

drought (n.) 乾旱
The earth is cracked and vegetation is withered. If the drought continues, even people will suffer.

地裂了，植物也荒蕪了。如果乾旱持續，連人類都要受罪。

eruption (n.) 爆發
In Indionesia, hundreds of people were evacuated because of the eruption of a volcano.

在印尼，因為一座火山爆發，數百人被撤離。

問題 098 解答 (A) floated 提出

解答 媒體對於這件嚴重的飛機失事**提出**了很多解釋。

選項 (A) 提出 (B) 取回 (C) 背書

補充例句

retrieve (v.) 取回
The black box was finally retrieved from the ocean two weeks after the crash.

黑盒子終於在飛機失事的兩個星期後被取回。

endorse (v.) 背書、代言
The company paid a million to the famous model to endorse their new perfume.

這間公司付了一百萬給這個有名的模特兒來為他們的新香水代言。

問題 099

One of the tasks of the Judicial Reform committee is to _____ a constitutional amendment.

        (A) interfere

        (B) install

        (C) initiate

問題 100

Our company has accepted _____ for the damage to the cargo.

        (A) bribery

        (B) capacity

        (C) liability

問題 099 解答 (C) initiate 創始、開始執行

解答 司法改革委員會的任務之一是**開始**一項憲法的修訂。

選項 (A) 干預、干涉 (B) 安裝、設置 (C) 創始、開始執行

補充例句

interfere (v.) 干預、干涉
I don't think it's kosher for us to interfere in their domestic problems.

對我們而言，我不認為介入他們的家庭問題是合宜的。

install (v.) 安裝、設置
Could you find time to come over and help me install my computer?

你可以找時間過來幫我安裝電腦嗎？

問題 100 解答 (C) liability 賠償責任

解答 我們的公司接受貨物損害的**賠償責任**。

選項 (A) 賄賂 (B) 產量 (C) 賠償責任

補充例句

bribery (n.) 賄賂
The candidate was convicted of bribery.

這位候選人被判有賄賂罪行。

capacity (n.) 產量
We have the excess capacity in manufacturing industry.

我們在製造業中有多餘的生產力。

The manager has approved our request and the accounting department will _____ the funds for the research project.

       (A) refer

       (B) allocate

       (C) certify

問題 102

With the most popular basketball player's _____ , the product will definitely sell like hot cakes.

       (A) endorsement

       (B) endowment

       (C) engagement

解答 經理已核准我們的申請，會計部門會針對我們的研究計畫**提撥**經費。

選項 (A) 提到、介紹　(B) 分派、分配　(C) 證實、證明

補充例句

refer (v.) 提到、介紹
During our conversation, he referred some useful books for my research.

在談話中，他提到了幾本對我的研究有幫助的書籍。

certify (v.) 證實、證明
The janitor certified at court that Mr. Smith was present at the crime scene on the day of the murder.

管理員在法庭證實史密斯先生在謀殺案當天有出現在案發現場。

解答 有最受歡迎的籃球選手**代言**，這個產品一定可以熱賣。

選項 (A) 為⋯背書　(B) 資助　(C) 約會

補充例句

endowment (n.) 捐贈、資助
My endowment policy is payable in 2020.

我的人壽保險在 2020 年就可以領回了。

engagement (n.) 約會
He has a prior engagement, so he can't come today.

他今天不能來，因為他事先有一個約會。

I forgot to bring my racket today. If we are going to play _____ later, I'll have to borrow yours.

(A) snooker

(B) squash

(C) archery

If we fail settle down the claim out of court, we will _____ a claim against them.

(A) lambast

(B) litigate

(C) locate

解答 我今天忘記帶球拍。如果我們待會兒要打**壁球**，我需要借用你的球拍。

選項 (A) 撞球　(B) 壁球　(C) 射箭

補充例句

snooker (n.) 撞球
In recent years, snooker has become a very popular after-school activity for teenagers.

近幾年來，撞球已經變成很受青少年歡迎的課後活動。

archery (n.) 射箭
The first time I tried archery, I couldn't even hold the bow firmly. But now, I'm very good at it.

我初次嘗試射箭，我幾乎無法穩定握好弓。但現在我已很擅長射箭了。

解答 如果我們無法在庭外和解，我們就要對他們**提出訴訟**。

選項 (A) 抨擊　(B) 打官司　(C) 把位置設在…

補充例句

lambast (v.) 抨擊
His team was lambasted for not performing well in the game.

他的團隊因為在比賽中表現不佳而飽受抨擊。

locate (v.) 把位置設在…
The company wants to locate the factory in China.

這間公司想要把工廠設在中國。

問題 105

I can't accept this _____ antique from you. It's way too valuable to be my birthday gift.

(A) genuine

(B) frigid

(C) erudite

問題 106

The professor was severely _____ and dismissed for his unprofessional conduct.

(A) censured

(B) composed

(C) concocted

問題 105 解答 (A) genuine 名符其實的

解答 我不能接受你這份**名符其實的**古董。對於一份生日禮物而言，它太貴重了。

選項 (A) 名符其實的　(B) 冷漠的　(C) 博學的

補充例句

frigid (adj.) 寒冷的
As a result of global warming, we haven't been experiencing a frigid weather for several years.

由於全球暖化，我們已經有好幾年沒有體驗到嚴寒的天氣了。

erudite (adj.) 博學的
Mr. Nelson is one of the most erudite professors in our school.

尼爾森先生是我們學校最博學的教授。

問題 106 解答 (A) censured 譴責

解答 這位教授因為不專業的行為，被嚴厲地**譴責**並解職。

選項 (A) 譴責　(B) 組成　(C) 編造

補充例句

compose (v.) 組成
Water is composed of oxygen and hydrogen.

水是由氧和氫組成的。

concoct (v.) 編造
In order to escape from the boring meeting, he concocted an excuse.

為了避開無聊的會議，他編造了一個藉口。

問題 107

The company has just bought a new operation system to _____ the old one.

      (A) compromise

      (B) supersede

      (C) subsidize

問題 108

In this department, there are serious penalties for failing to _____ with regulations.

      (A) clarify

      (B) classify

      (C) comply

解答 公司已經買了一個新的作業系統來**替換**舊系統。

選項 (A) 妥協 (B) 代替、接替 (C) 資助

補充例句

compromise (v.) 妥協
The politician compromised his integrity for obtaining the support of the most influential union leader.

這位政客犧牲了他的正直，以換取最有影響力的政黨領袖的支持。

subsidize (v.) 資助
The arts in our country are in need of being subsidized.

我們國內的藝術是需要被資助的。

解答 在這個部門，沒有**遵守**規定會有嚴厲的處罰。

選項 (A) 澄清 (B) 分類 (C) 遵守

補充例句

clarify (v.) 澄清
The forensic detective's explanation clarified the mystery.

那位法醫學偵探的解釋揭開了謎底。

classify (v.) 分類
The books in the library are classified according to subject.

圖書館的書是依照科目來分類的。

It's now the consensus among all members of United Nations to _____ nuclear weapons.

(A) ban

(B) confine

(C) deprive

We have made a down _____ on our first apartment.

(A) payment

(B) procurement

(C) proliferation

問題 109 解答 (A) ban 禁止

解答 **禁止**使用核武現在已經是所有聯合國會員的共識。

選項 (A) 禁止　(B) 限制　(C) 剝奪

補充例句

confine (v.) 限制
The editor in chief asked me to confine my efforts to finishing the book first.

主編要求我盡全力先完成這本書。

deprive (v.) 剝奪
The mother deprived her son of candy for he's already been suffering from cavities.

這位母親不准她兒子吃糖，因為他已經有蛀牙之苦了。

問題 110 解答 (A) payment 付款

解答 我們用延遲**付款**的方式購買了我們的第一間公寓。

選項 (A) 付款　(B) 採購　(C) 擴散

補充例句

procurement (n.) 採購
The buyer is responsible for the procurement of military supplies.

採購者負責軍中物品的採購。

proliferation (n.) 擴散
The proliferation of weapons of mass destruction is a cause for concern.

大規模毀滅性武器的擴散是一個令人擔憂的原因。

問題 111

My science teacher has found some natural ways to _____ mosquitoes.

> (A) repel
>
> (B) restrain
>
> (C) admonish

問題 112

Their company has a(n) _____ for a marketing director.

> (A) currency
>
> (B) expectancy
>
> (C) vacancy

解答 我的科學老師發現了一些天然的**防**蚊方法。

選項 (A) 拒絕、排斥　(B) 克制、約束　(C) 警告、責備

補充例句

restrain (v.) 克制、約束
I can't restrain her from talking as it's like air to her.
我無法約束她不說話，因為說話對她而言就像空氣般重要。

admonish (v.) 警告、責備
Don't let me admonish you about your obligations as a student again. If you are late again, I'll send you to the principle's office directly.
別讓我再次警告你作為學生的職責。如果你再遲到，我會直接請你進校長室。

解答 他們公司有一個行銷主任的**職缺**。

選項 (A) 貨幣　(B) 期望　(C) 職缺

補充例句

currency (n.) 貨幣
Sterling has been one of the strongest currencies in the world.
英鎊一直是世界上最強的貨幣之一。

expectancy (n.) 期待
The life expectancy gap between two sexes in many countries is widening.
世界上男女平均壽命的差距一直在變大。

問題 113

The engineer reminded us that computer errors are a common _____.

        (A) insurance

        (B) occurrence

        (C) endurance

問題 114

Her latest album _____ her earlier songs.

        (A) agitates

        (B) appeals

        (C) incorporates

解答 工程師提醒我們，電腦錯誤是很常**發生**的事。

選項 (A) 保險 (B) 發生 (C) 忍受

補充例句

insurance (n.) 保險
Car insurance premiums have gone up this month.
這個月車子的保險費提高了。

endurance (n.) 忍受
The run in Sahara tested Mr. Lin's endurance to the limit
在撒哈拉沙漠的跑步挑戰了林先生的忍耐度到極限。

解答 她最新的唱片**收錄**了她較早期的歌曲。

選項 (A) 擾亂 (B) 呼籲、懇求 (C) 加入

補充例句

agitates (agitate) (v.) 擾亂
I'm now in the middle of something. Please leave me alone and don't agitate me.
我現在正在忙某件事。請讓我獨處並且不要打擾我。

appeal (v.) 呼籲、懇求
The college appealed to its alumni for funds to reconstruct their classroom buildings.
這間大學呼籲它的校友捐助基金幫助教室大樓的整建。

問題 115

Travelers who want to visit that famous spring resort has to take a _____ because the road was destroyed during the typhoon.

(A) detour

(B) embark

(C) redeem

問題 116

The expedition through the Sahara desert was _____ with difficulties.

(A) caught

(B) drought

(C) fraught

解答 要去知名溫泉遊玩的旅客必須**繞道**，因為道路在颱風期間被摧毀了。

選項 (A) 繞道　(B) 搭乘、著手　(C) 付清、贖回

補充例句

embark (v.) 搭乘、著手

After planning for three years, Blair finally embarked on his journey on Sunday.

在計畫了三年後，布萊爾終於在星期天展開了旅程。

redeem (v.) 付清、贖回

My parents worked so hard to redeem the mortgage of our house.

我的父母工作得十分辛苦來付清我們房屋的貸款。

解答 穿越沙哈拉沙漠的探險**充滿**困難。

選項 (A) 抓住　(B) 乾旱　(C) 充滿

補充例句

caught (p.p.) 抓住

It's the problem between you and him. I don't want to get caught in the middle.

這是你和他之間的問題，我不想夾在中間。

drought (n.) 乾旱

The dry weather caused a serious drought in the area.

乾燥的天氣在這個區域造成嚴重的乾旱。

When you speak, please avoid adopting that
_____ tone. You sound like you distrust me.

(A) subsidiary

(B) superficial

(C) skeptical

They _____ themselves in different types of
leisure activities on holidays.

(A) indulge

(B) auction

(C) fluctuate

解答 當你說話時，請不要用**懷疑的**語氣。你聽起來並不信任我。

選項 (A) 輔助的、次要的 (B) 膚淺的 (C) 不信的、懷疑的

補充例句

subsidiary (adj.) 輔助的、次要的
As this is a subsidiary issue, the chairman doesn't want us to spend too much time on it.

由於這是次要的議題，主席不希望我們花太多時間在上面。

superficial (adj.) 膚淺的
Don't be so superficial. Besides money, there're so many other important things in life.

別這麼膚淺。金錢之外，人生還有其他重要議題膚淺。

解答 他們在假日**盡情享受**不同形式的休閒活動。

選項 (A) 盡情享受 (B) 拍賣 (C) 起伏不定

補充例句

auction (v.) 拍賣
The precious diamond necklace was auctioned last Friday.

這條珍貴的鑽石項鍊上星期五被拍賣了。

fluctuate (v.) 浮動、起伏不定
Their sales figures have fluctuated over the last two years.

他們的銷售業績這一兩年一直起伏不定。

The mother was so heartbroken when she saw her only son _____ and get involved in drug dealing.

(A) abide

(B) resolve

(C) deteriorate

The preliminary discussions between the two leaders were _____ in secrecy.

(A) valid

(B) veiled

(C) void

問題 119 解答　(C) deteriorate 使惡化

解答　當這位母親看到她的獨子**變壞**並且涉入販毒時，
她傷心透了。

選項　(A) 容忍　(B) 解決　(C) 使惡化

補充例句

abide (v.) 容忍
You know I can't abide dishonesty. Why did you still lie to me?
你知道我無法容忍不誠實。你為什麼還要對我撒謊呢？

resolve (v.) 解決
There's no way we can resolve Judy's problem unless she tells
us what happened.
除非茱蒂告訴我們發生了什麼事，否則我們無法幫她解決問題。

問題 120 解答　(B) veiled 隱藏的

解答　兩國元首之間的初步討論在**祕密**中進行。

選項　(A) 有效的　(B) 隱藏的　(C) 無效的

補充例句

valid (adj.) 有效的
That passenger doesn't possess a valid passport so she can't
check in.
那位旅客並未持有一本有效的護照，所以她無法報到。

void (adj.) 無效的
It was a shock to them because the court declared the contract
void.
他們相當震驚，因為法院宣告這紙合約無效。

The company is working on a science _____
to persuade consumers accept their product.

      (A) hypothesis

      (B) colloquy

      (C) facilitate

The government encourages all employees to
join a _____.

      (A) union

      (B) venue

      (C) fraud

問題 121 解答　(A) hypothesis 學說、理論

解答　公司正在發展一個科學上的**理論**來說服消費者接受他們的產品。

選項　(A) 學說、理論　(B) 談話　(C) 促進、幫助

補充例句

colloquy (n.) 談話
The purpose of this colloquy was meant to find out the truth.
這個談話的目的是要找出事實。

facilitate (v.) 促進、幫助
Shirley offers us her brilliant ideas to facilitate our market share.
雪莉提供我們非常好的意見來幫助我們的市場佔有率。

問題 122 解答　(A) union 工會

解答　政府鼓勵所有的員工都參加**工會**。

選項　(A) 工會　(B) 會場　(C) 詐欺

補充例句

venue (n.) 會場
The hotel is a popular venue for wedding receptions.
這間飯店是很受歡迎的婚宴會場。

fraud (n.) 詐騙
The bank clerk got a 10-year sentence for fraud.
這個銀行行員因為詐欺被判十年有期徒刑。

問題 123

Julia is such a(an) _____ shopper and she just can't control herself.

      (A) hectic

      (B) obscure

      (C) reckless

問題 124

One of the most frightening natural _____ is an earthquake.

      (A) scenes

      (B) diseases

      (C) hazards

解答 茱莉亞是個**衝動的**購物者而且她從來無法控制自己。

選項 (A) 緊張忙碌的　(B) 不清楚的　(C) 魯莽的

補充例句

hectic (adj.) 緊張忙碌的
This has been a hectic week for me and I don't think I'll be able to visit another customer.
這週對我而言真是忙碌。我想我不能再多拜訪一個客戶了。

obscure (adj.) 不清楚的
We need to talk about this sentence as there shouldn't be anything obscure in the contract.
我們需要對這個句子做討論，在合約裡不該有任何不清楚的地方。

解答 地震是最恐怖的天然**危險**災害之一 。

選項 (A) 場景　(B) 疾病　(C) 危險

補充例句

scene (n.) 場景
A knife and a gun were found at the crime scene.
一把刀和槍在犯罪現場被找到。

disease (n.) 疾病
Many diseases are caused by bacteria on our hands.
很多疾病是由於我們手上的細菌所引起的。

It's _____ of you to confront the teacher on the classroom rules.

       (A) aloof

       (B) adjustable

       (C) audacious

The Kiwi bird is a bird _____ to New Zealand.

       (A) indigenous

       (B) indifferent

       (C) invisible

問題 125 解答 (C) audacious 勇敢的、大膽的

解答　妳真是**大膽**敢跟老師在教室規定這點上槓上。

選項　(A) 冷漠的　(B) 可調整的　(C) 勇敢的、大膽的

補充例句　請看下面其他兩個字彙的例句

aloof (adj.) 冷漠的
This is an aloof area. Neighbors here don't greet each other.
這是個冷漠的區域。這裡的鄰居見面是不打招呼的。

adjustable (adj.) 可調整的
Don't worry about the work schedule because it's adjustable.
別擔心這份工作時間表，它是可以調整的。

問題 126 解答 (A) indigenous 本地的

解答　奇異鳥是一種紐西蘭**當地的**鳥類。

選項　(A) 本地的　(B) 漠不關心的　(C) 看不見的

補充例句

indifferent (adj) 漠不關心的
The new boss looks cold and indifferent.
新老闆看起來冷酷且漠不關心。

invisible (adj.) 無形的、看不見的
Tourism is one of the most profitable invisible imports.
觀光業是獲利最高的無形輸入當中的一種。

Where did you _____ this idea from? I can't say it's the best but it will definitely work.

(A) demolish

(B) evolve

(C) impose

This is the best price I can _____ you.

(A) estimate

(B) deduct

(C) quote

解答 你們從哪兒得出這個想法的？我不能說它是最棒的，
但是它絕對可行。

選項 (A) 推翻、毀壞　(B) 進化、得出　(C) 徵稅、加於

補充例句

demolish (v.) 推翻、毀壞
The results of his research demolished many theories.

他的研究結果推翻了許多理論。

impose (v.) 徵稅、加於
Please do not try to impose your preference on me. I will not
go for your choice of color.

請不要嘗試要叫我接受你的喜好，我不會喜歡你對顏色的選擇的。

解答 這是我能給你最好的**報價**。

選項 (A) 估計　(B) 減少　(C) 報價

補充例句

estimate (v.) 估計
They estimated that it would take 10 years to complete the
tunnel.

他們估計要花十年才能完成隧道建造。

deduct (v.) 減少
Tax will be deducted from your salary per month.

稅會在每個月從你的薪水中扣除。

As she _____ her knee when she tripped at the door, we advised her to have it taken care of right away.

(A) scraped

(B) squashed

(C) dilated

If you are not satisfied with your purchase, our company _____ to refund your money.

(A) elaborates

(B) guarantees

(C) economizes

問題 129 解答 (A) scraped 刮傷

解答 她在門邊跌倒**刮傷**了膝蓋，我們建議她要馬上處理。

選項 (A) 刮傷　 (B) 壓扁　 (C) 擴大

補充例句

squashed (squash) (v.) 壓扁
Would you please stay out of the garden? You were about to squash the flowers.

你們可以避開花園嗎？你們差點要踩扁那些花了。

dilated (dilate) (v.) 擴大
This child's pupil dilated. Did you put drops in his eyes?

這孩子的瞳孔放大。你剛剛幫他點了眼藥水了嗎？

問題 130 解答 (B) guarantees 保證

解答 如果你不滿意你的貨物，我們公司會**保證**退錢。

選項 (A) 說明　 (B) 保證　 (C) 節約

補充例句 請看下面其他兩個字彙的例句

elaborate (v.) 說明
Would you like to elaborate on the details of your plan?

你要將你的計畫細節說明一下嗎？

economize (v.) 節約
The company decides to economize by reducing the member of the staff.

公司決定要減少公司成員來節省金錢。

問題 131

He's got a(an) _____ mind and that makes him the key player in our debate team.

    (A) vigilant

    (B) obsequious

    (C) incisive

問題 132

Mr. Smith believes that this is an agreement that will be for our _____ benefit.

    (A) regular

    (B) mutual

    (C) adamant

問題 131 解答 (C) incisive 尖刻的、銳利的

解答 他有個非常**敏銳的**思緒，因此他是我們辯論隊裡的主要戰將。

選項 (A) 警覺性的　(B) 諂媚的　(C) 尖刻的、銳利的

補充例句

vigilant (adj.) 警覺性的
You have to be vigilant when going out alone at night as this is a dangerous area.

這是個危險的區域，所以當你在晚上單獨出門時要保持警覺。

obsequious (adj.) 諂媚的
The submissive servant just made an obsequious bow to the master.

這個順從的侍者對主人諂媚地鞠了個躬。

問題 132 解答 (B) mutual 互相的

解答 史密斯先生相信這是對於**雙方**都有利的協議。

選項 (A) 固定的　(B) 互相的　(C) 堅定的

補充例句

regular (adj.) 固定的、正常的
We have been meeting on a regular basis.

我們固定見面。

adamant (adj.) 堅定的
We tried to persuade him not to resign but he was adamant.

我們試著說服他不要辭職，但是他相當堅定。

The weather is _____ frigid and there were already three people frozen to death.

        (A) approximately

        (B) definitely

        (C) extraordinary

The celebrity's company _____ heavy losses in its second year.

        (A) occurred

        (B) reassured

        (C) incurred

問題 133 解答 (C) extraordinary 異常地

解答 天氣**異常**酷寒，已經有三個人被凍死了。

選項 (A) 大約 (B) 肯定地 (C) 異常地

補充例句

approximately (adv.) 大約
The survey showed that there were approximately ten thousand people taking this test this year.

調查顯示今年大約有一萬人參加這個考試。

definitely (adv.) 肯定地
I'll definitely go to my grandmother's ninety- year- old birthday party.

我絕對會參加我祖母的九十歲生日宴會。

問題 134 解答 (C) incurred 遭受

解答 這間名人的公司在第二年**遭受**到嚴重的損失。

選項 (A) 發生 (B) 再確認 (C) 遭受

補充例句

occur (v.) 發生
It has never occurred to me that I would win the first prize.

我從來沒有想過我會贏得頭獎。

reassure (v.) 使放心
He was worried that his performance wasn't good enough but his supervisor reassured him about it.

他擔心他的表現不夠好，但是他的主管讓他放心。

問題 135

Have you figured out any possible solution that doesn't _____ the patents?

        (A) assemble

        (B) infringe

        (C) obstruct

問題 136

The film has been a success, thanks to the _____ of all of our staff.

        (A) injunction

        (B) dedication

        (C) extortion

問題 135 解答 (B) infringe 破壞、違反

解答 妳有想出來任何不會**違反**專利的解決方法嗎？

選項 (A) 收集、裝配 (B) 破壞、違反 (C) 阻擋、遮斷

補充例句

assemble (v.) 收集、裝配
Have you finished assembling information for the report you've been working on?

妳完成了爲妳目前進行中的報告訊息的收集嗎？

obstruct (v.) 阻擋、遮斷
The debris from the eruption obstructed the road.

火山爆發的殘骸阻斷了道路。

問題 136 解答 (B) dedication 貢獻

解答 這部電影很成功，要感謝所有的工作人員的**貢獻**。

選項 (A) 禁制令 (B) 貢獻 (C) 勒索

補充例句

injunction (n.) 禁制令
The court granted him an injunction to prevent the story being published.

法院對他下禁制令，以避免這則故事被刊載。

extortion (n.) 勒索
The policeman was found guilty of extortion.

這個警察被判有勒索罪。

Samuel is going to make a _____ on his parents' anniversary.

(A) compassionate

(B) complimentary

(C) commensurate

_____ industries provide services rather than selling or making products.

(A) Tertiary

(B) Preliminary

(C) Primary

問題 137 解答 (B) complimentary 恭維、稱讚

解答 山繆要在他父母的結婚紀念日致**頌辭**。

選項 (A) 有同情心的 (B) 恭維、稱讚 (C) 同量的、相當的

補充例句

compassionate (adj.) 有同情心的
My mother is so compassionate that she donates money to the charity regularly.

我的母親十分有同情心，所以她定期地捐錢給慈善機構。

commensurate (adj.) 同量的、相當的
Your paycheck should be commensurate with the amount of time worked.

你的薪水應該與你的工作時數是相當的。

問題 138 解答 (A) tertiary 服務性的

解答 **服務**業提供服務而不是販賣或是製造產品。

選項 (A) 服務性的 (B) 初步的 (C) 主要的

補充例句

preliminary (adj.) 初步的
The preliminary analysis showed that the company's failure was caused by impulsive investment.

初步分析顯示這間公司失敗的原因是衝動的投資所導致。

primary (adj.) 主要的
The mayor stressed that dealing with crime is the police's primary concern.

市長強調處理犯罪是警方最主要的考量。

The manager was asked to make an _____ demonstration in front of the crowds.

   (A) incidental

   (B) mandatory

   (C) impromptu

Marketing is familiar _____ to my coworker and his team.

   (A) exposure

   (B) territory

   (C) award

問題 139 解答 (C) impromptu 即席的

解答 經理被要求對群眾做一場**即席**示範。

選項 (A) 意外的 (B) 命令的、強制的 (C) 即席的

補充例句

incidental (adj.) 意外的

There were several incidental expenses last month and I even need to borrow money to counteract it.

上個月有好幾筆意外的開銷，我甚至必須去借錢來應付。

mandatory (adj.) 命令的、強制的

It's mandatory at my school that all students have to take two years of English class.

在我們的學校，學生被強制要求上兩年的英文課。

問題 140 解答 (B) territory 領域

解答 行銷對我的同事和他的團隊而言是很熟悉的**領域**。

選項 (A) 暴露 (B) 領域 (C) 獎品

補充例句

exposure (n.) 暴露

After three hours of exposure to sunlight, we all had serious sunburn.

暴露在陽光底下三個小時後，我們全部都有嚴重的曬傷。

award (n.) 獎品

The award for this year's best actress went to Sandra Bullock.

今年最佳女主角為珊卓布拉克。

問題 141

The only thing he likes to talk about is how
_____ he is as a successful banker.

        (A) worn-out

        (B) well-off

        (C) cast-off

問題 142

The special offer is _____ to members of
this bookstore.

        (A) inclusive

        (B) exclusive

        (C) extensive

解答 他唯一喜歡談的事情是他自己是多麼**富有**的成功銀行家。

選項 (A) 穿破了的 (B) 十分富有的 (C) 被捨棄的

補充例句

worn-out (adj.) 穿破了的
Why don't you get rid of those shoes? They are all worn-out.
你爲什麼不把那些鞋子丟掉呢？它們都被穿壞了。

cast-off (adj.) 被捨棄的
When we were children, we used to wear other people's cast-off clothes to save money.
當我們還是孩子時，我們都穿別人不要的衣服來省錢。

解答 特別的價格只限於本書店的會員。

選項 (A) 包含的 (B) 專用的 (C) 廣泛的

補充例句

inclusive (adj.) 包含的
She won a 2-week inclusive holiday in Bali Island.
她贏得到巴里島的兩週套裝假期。

extensive (adj.) 廣泛的
The hurricane caused extensive damage all over the country.
颶風造成全國大規模的災害。

問題 143

In order to improve my English writing ability, I write two English _____ a week.

(A) oppressions

(B) deportations

(C) compositions

問題 144

We need to try harder to reduce our _____.

(A) options

(B) overviews

(C) overheads

問題 143 解答 (C) compositions 寫作、樂曲

解答 為了增進我的英文寫作能力，我每週寫兩篇英文**作文**。

選項 (A) 壓抑、壓迫　(B) 驅逐出境　(C) 寫作、樂曲

補充例句

oppression (n.) 壓抑、壓迫
After years of oppression, the people finally revolted against the government.

在多年的壓迫後，人民終於反抗政府。

deportation (n.) 驅逐出境
There will be a possibility of deportation if your visa is expired.

如果你的簽證過期，那就有可能被驅逐出境。

問題 144 解答 (C) overheads 固定開銷、經常費用

解答 我們應該努力點來減少我們的**經常開支**。

選項 (A) 選擇　(B) 概要　(C) 固定開銷、經常費用

補充例句

option (n.) 選擇
You have two options reduce spending or to increase income.

你有兩個選擇：減少支出或是增加收入。

overview (n.) 概要
The boss gave us an overview of the company's plans for the coming year.

老闆給我們明年公司計畫的概要。

問題 145

She's such a (an) _____ person who's never afraid of any challenges or difficulties.

(A) outrageous

(B) courageous

(C) furious

問題 146

The coffee shop owner rents the house but she _____ the basement to a company.

(A) sublets

(B) submits

(C) subscribes

問題 145 解答 (B) courageous 英勇的、勇敢的

解答 她是個很**勇敢**的人，從來不怕挑戰和困難。

選項 (A) 無法容忍的 (B) 英勇的、勇敢的 (C) 暴怒的

補充例句

outrageous (adj.) 無法容忍的
I just can't stand your outrageous cruelty to your pet. Animals are entitled to be treated nicely.

我無法忍受你對寵物過分殘酷的行為，動物有權利被溫柔地對待。

furious (adj.) 暴怒的
Mr. Smith became furious when he found that his legally-parked was towed away.

當史密斯先生發現他合法停好的車被拖走時暴怒了起來。

問題 146 解答 (A) sublets 分租

解答 咖啡店老闆把房子租下來，但是她把地下室**分租**給一間公司。

選項 (A) 分租 (B) 呈遞 (C) 訂閱

補充例句

submit (v.) 呈遞、提交
The final decision will be submitted this Friday.

最後的決定在這個星期五會被提交出去。

subscribe (v.) 訂閱
We have subscribed to some sports channels.

我們已經訂閱了一些運動頻道。

問題 147

The company can't _____ people for no reason. If they do, you can sue them and get it justified.

(A) dismiss

(B) retire

(C) apply

問題 148

Don't forget to _____ your license which is going to be expired next week.

(A) contact

(B) indemnify

(C) renew

問題 147 解答　(A) dismiss 解職

解答　公司不可以無故**解雇**人。如果他們這麼做，你可以控告他們取得平反。

選項　(A) 解職　(B) 退休　(C) 申請

補充例句

retire (v.) 退休
No matter how old their staff is, this company never forces anybody to retire.

不論他們的員工多老，這家公司都不會強迫任何人退休。

apply (v.) 申請
Once I knew there was a spot in that company, I sent my resume out to apply for the job.

我一知道那間公司有空缺，我馬上就寄出我的履歷表申請工作。

問題 148 解答　(C) renew 更新

解答　不要忘記**更新**你的執照，下星期就要過期了。

選項　(A) 聯繫　(B) 保障　(C) 更新

補充例句

contact (v.) 聯繫
You can always contact me by phone or email.

你隨時可以用電話或是電子郵件和我聯繫。

indemnify (v.) 保障、賠償
The insurance doesn't indemnify the house against earthquake.

保險並沒有賠償地震對房屋造成的損害。

I _____ my ankle when playing basketball
school yesterday.

      (A) twisted

      (B) bumped

      (C) broke

He is in short of cash this month so he asks for a
(an) _____ on his wages.

      (A) recovery

      (B) advance

      (C) schedule

問題 149 解答 (A) twisted 扭到

解答 我昨天打籃球時，我**扭傷**我的腳踝。

選項 (A) 扭到 (B) 撞到 (C) 碎裂

補充例句

bump (v.) 撞到
Though the boy often bumps his head, he doesn't cry .
即使這個男孩常撞到頭，他都不哭。

break (v.) 碎裂
James broke his arms in that car accident. Fortunately the driver who hit him didn't run away.

詹姆士在車禍時弄斷了手臂，幸運的是撞他的司機沒有跑走。

問題 150 解答 (B) advance 預付款

解答 他這個月缺現金，所以他要求**預支薪資**。

選項 (A) 復甦 (B) 預付款 (C) 進度表

補充例句

recovery (n.) 復甦
Economic recovery was rather slow after the recession in the world.

全球經濟不景氣後的經濟復甦相當慢。

schedule (n.) 進度表
All international flights depart on schedule today.
今日所有國際行班都按照時間表起飛。

問題 151

This winter is outrageously cold. Just yesterday, my fingers were _____ with cold.

    (A) senseless

    (B) indifferent

    (C) numb

問題 152

Henry is _____ at the bank so he must pay off his overdraft.

    (A) oversold

    (B) overstocked

    (C) overdrawn

解答 這個冬天出奇的冷。就在昨天,我的手指頭因為過冷而**麻木**。

選項 (A) 無意義的 (B) 不感興趣的 (C) 失去感覺的、麻木的

補充例句

senseless (adj.) 無意義的

The citizens were disappointed by the senseless speech the mayor gave yesterday.

市民對市長昨天所做的沒有內容的演講感到失望。

indifferent (adj.) 不感興趣的

People here are so art indifferent and that really bothers me.

這裡的人對藝術如此冷感真的讓我不舒服。

解答 亨利的銀行帳戶透支了,所以他必須支付他所**透支**的款項。

選項 (A) 超賣 (B) 庫存過多 (C) 透支

補充例句

oversell (v.) 銷售過多

The concert tickets are already oversold.

演唱會的票已經超賣了。

overstock (v.) 存貨過多

The supermarket was overstocked with fresh produce.

這間超市有過多新鮮農產品的存貨。

問題 153

Please do not _____ the proceeding of this investigation.

      (A) restore

      (B) recruit

      (C) retard

問題 154

The system in this country provides a useful tax _____ for his company.

      (A) shelter

      (B) return

      (C) haven

問題 153 解答　(C) retard 妨礙

解答　請不要**妨礙**到調查的進行。

選項　(A) 恢復　(B) 聘用　(C) 妨礙

補充例句

restore (v.) 恢復
I just called the power company and they confirmed that the electricity will be restored in two hours.

我剛剛打給電力公司，他們確認在兩小時內會恢復電力。

recruit (v.) 聘用
Do you know if your company is recruiting? I'm now between jobs and I'm interested in your company.

你知道你們公司有在徵人嗎？我目前失業，而且我很想進你們公司。

問題 154 解答　(A) shelter 庇護

解答　這國家的制度提供了他的公司一個合法的避稅手段。

選項　(A) 庇護　(B) 歸還　(C) 避難所

補充例句

return (n.) 歸還
If you are self-employed, you need to complete a tax return.

如果你是自由業，你必須填寫報稅單。

haven (n.) 避難所
Some countries are tax havens such as Singapore and Bahamas.

有些國家是低稅國家，像是新加坡和巴哈馬。

問題 155

I think we need to _____ to the plan as we all think it will work.

(A) arouse

(B) adhere

(C) audit

問題 156

All authors were _____ in alphabetical order.

(A) ranked

(B) rallied

(C) recouped

問題 155 解答　(B) adhere 堅持、黏附

解答　我認為既然我們都認為這個計畫可行，我們就應該**堅持**。

選項　(A) 引起　(B) 堅持、黏附　(C) 會計稽查、審計

補充例句

arouse (v.) 引起
It's already late at night and I certainly believe that you don't want to arouse too much attention.

現在很晚了，而且我相信你必然不想引起太多注意。

audit (v.) 會計稽查、審計
The company auditor will start auditing our division tomorrow.

公司稽查專員在明天要開始我們部門的稽查。

問題 156 解答　(A) ranked 排列

解答　所有的作者都是依照字母順序**排列**。

選項　(A) 排列　(B) 回升　(C) 補償

補充例句

rally (v.) 回升
On Monday, the share price rallied significantly again.

星期一股票價格再度顯著地回升。

recoup (v.) 補償、償還
The company seems unable to recoup their losses during the economic crisis.

這間公司看起來無法償還他們在經濟危機期間的損失。

問題 157

Did you notice that there wasn't _____ among these representatives?

   (A) commend

   (B) commence

   (C) concord

問題 158

About 20 people were arrested while _____ outside the US embassy.

   (A) haggling

   (B) malfunctioning

   (C) picketing

解答 你有注意到他們這幾位代表並沒有**共識**嗎？

選項 (A) 讚揚、推薦 (B) 開始 (C) 協調、一致

補充例句

commend (v.) 讚揚、推薦

It was nice of you to commend Janet to me. She's such a nice secretary.

妳真好介紹珍娜給我。她是非常棒的祕書。

commence (v.) 開始

The meeting will commence in ten minutes and I'm still stuck in the traffic.

會議在十分鐘內要開始，而我還困在車陣中。

解答 大約二十個人在美國大使館外面**示威抗議**時被逮捕。

選項 (A) 殺價 (B) 故障 (C) 示威抗議

補充例句

haggle (v.) 討價還價

I haggled down the rent by about one fourth.

我把房租殺價四分之一。

malfunction (v.) 發生故障

Nobody knows what caused the rocket to malfunction.

沒有人知道什麼導致火箭發生故障。

問題 159

This _____ task only took him a few minutes to finish.

(A) deviant

(B) elusive

(C) facile

問題 160

Larry raised several questions in the meeting but they are not _____ to our project.

(A) vacant

(B) pertinent

(C) affluent

解答　這個**容易至極**的任務只花了他幾分鐘就完成了。

選項　(A) 不正常的　(B) 難懂的　(C) 輕而易舉的

補充例句

deviant (adj.) 不正常的

His deviant behavior was mainly from his miserable childhood.

他的不正常行為大部分應歸咎於他悲慘的童年。

elusive (adj.) 難懂的

Love is something that can be very elusive. There are people who never know what love is for their whole life.

愛情是非常不容易懂的。有人終其一生不懂什麼是愛情。

解答　賴瑞在會議上提了幾個問題，不過它們跟我們的計畫
無關。

選項　(A) 空缺的　(B) 有關的　(C) 富裕的

補充例句

vacant (adj.) 空缺的

The position of our company manager has been vacant for three months.

我們公司經理的職缺已經空了三個月。

affluent (adj.) 富裕的

He was born in a rich family so he has an affluent lifestyle.

他出生在一個富有的家庭，所以他有一個富裕的生活方式。

Note

看不懂的單字
不要再猜了好嗎？

國家圖書館出版品預行編目資料

1日1分鐘 新多益必考單字問題集 / 劉慧如，鄭苔英編著.
初版． -- 臺北市 . 書泉，2010. 11
　　　面；　　公分
ISBN 978-986-121-632-4（平裝附光碟片）

1. 多益測驗 2. 詞彙

805. 1895　　　　　　　　　　　　　　99017587

3AN3 1日1分鐘 01

1日1分鐘 新多益必考單字問題集

作　者：劉慧如　鄭苔英
發行人：楊榮川
總編輯：龐君豪
主　編：魏　巍
封面設計：羅靜琪
出版者：書泉出版社
地址：106 台北市大安區和平東路二段 339 號 4 樓
電話：(02)2705-5066　傳真：(02)2706-6100
網址：http：//www.wunan.com.tw
電子郵件：shuchuan@shuchuan.com.tw
劃撥帳號：01303853
戶名：書泉出版社
總經銷：聯寶國際文化事業有限公司
電話：(02) 2695-4083
地址：台北縣汐止市康寧街 169 巷 27 號 8 樓
法律顧問：元貞聯合法律事務所　張澤平律師
出版日期：2010 年 11 月 初版一刷
定價：新台幣 149 元

ESSENTIAL TOEIC VOCABULARY

ESSENTIAL TOEIC VOCABULARY
ESSENTIAL TOEIC VOCABULARY
ESSENTIAL TOEIC VOCABULARY
ESSENTIAL TOEIC VOCABULARY
ESSENTIAL TOEIC VOCABULARY
ESSENTIAL TOEIC VOCABULARY
ESSENTIAL TOEIC VOCABULARY
ESSENTIAL TOEIC VOCABULARY
ESSENTIAL TOEIC VOCABULARY
ESSENTIAL TOEIC VOCABULARY
ESSENTIAL TOEIC VOCABULARY
ESSENTIAL TOEIC VOCABULARY
ESSENTIAL TOEIC VOCABULARY
ESSENTIAL TOEIC VOCABULARY
ESSENTIAL TOEIC VOCABULARY
ESSENTIAL TOEIC VOCABULARY

ESSENTIAL TOEIC VOCABULARY